PRAISE FOR GHOST WRITERS: THE HAUNTING OF LAKE LUCY

I loved it and I know my students will too! I'm excited it's a novel in verse. Since they love spooky, I think it's a great way to get them into the world of novels in verse too!

— CANDICE

I loved the way the author played w/words & poetic form, as well as letter writing. A mysteriously spooky setting & circumstance kept me turning the pages till the end!

— CHRISTIE

If you like kids' horror and novels-in-verse, I suspect you'll enjoy this book quite a bit!

— CHRISTIANA D.

This middle grade novel-in-verse was a delight to read from start to finish! Beautifully written and lyrical...with its exceptionally gorgeous cover, it will make a beautiful addition to any home, school, or library.

— STACEY B.

Wait a minute...a horror-mg-novel in verse?! Yes please!! This will be popular among kids who love scary stories but it will also help crack the door open for those kids that don't really like to read.

— CINDY S.

I'll bet my students would scoop this one right up!

— DESTINY L.

The story's descriptive detail, thoughtful verse, and the relationship between the siblings and the lake setting all contribute to its charm and mystery... It reminded me of the ghost stories we would share around campfires and the tales we would tell to one-up our friends.

— CHERYL

The Haunting of Lake Lucy is a fun fast paced ghost story filled with coded messages, strange happenings, a new and mysterious friendship, and a thriller-chiller conclusion. A most satisfying Ghost story.

— HAN NOLAN, NATIONAL BOOK AWARD WINNER AND AUTHOR OF RUNNING PAST DARK

Sandy Green's verse runs the gamut: free verse, rhyming couplets, some shape poetry, creative use of bolded letters as well as shaded portions of text. There is even an example of line palindrome. Her characters are clearly developed and the mystery grows with every chapter. Along with the ghostly storyline are subplots of making friends and getting along with siblings. Text is free of profanity, sexual content and violence. Ideal for grades 4-8.

— MELANIE

GHOST WRITERS

THE HAUNTING OF LAKE LUCY

HORROR IN VERSE

SANDY DEUTSCHER GREEN

For Gary, Olivia, and Andy
and
Blas Madera

SUMMER VACATION AT THE LAKE

On sparkling Lake Lucy
two giant rafts
bob in place
with invisible straps
tethered to underwater rocks

their hidden ties
tug at the bloated floats

I shift my feet
in the sand on the public beach
as bunches of kids jump and slide
on the rafts

I don't know anyone
but my twin sister
who never has trouble joining a group
like she's known them all her life
instead of a few days

the water shivers
from the breeze
me too

though the sun bakes my head

"Come on, Jayce!"
Evie throws her towel
and Mr. Crunch[1]
on our blanket
she plunges into the water
joins kids swarming
over the giant trampoline raft

I step into the warm waves
shade sleepy eyes
sand swirls around my ankles

my gaze runs along the roped area
with red and white bobbers
silent warnings:

> *Don't swim beyond these edges*
> *Don't go where you don't belong*
> *A ham sandwich would be nice right about now*

shake my head
fling away nonsense chats
with myself
when I don't get enough sleep

---

[1]**Mr. Crunch**

Stuffed blue lizard
three feet long
ring of green fluff
like a beard

Noah won him
at the fair
Evie's first crush
hence the name.

wade up to my waist
inhale the lake-y smell
fresh and faintly fishy
like air before rain

swim for the less crowded
blow-up slide raft
skim down a hundred times
with other kids
so fun

a good way to get away
from horse flies
pesky bugs who nip at arms and legs
like bad dreams
as if it's that easy
to wash away nightmares

Evie doggy-paddles to the slide:
"Try the trampoline, Jayce."

trade places with my twin
bounce with other kids around thirteen
like us

after a while
we stretch on the rubbery top
heads meeting in the middle
spokes on a gigantic bicycle wheel

"This is our first time at the lake. How long
have these rafts been here?"
I wonder out loud

"They were new last summer. I would know.
I come every year with my family,"
Crystal says

Blas from New York sits up
waves his hand at the beach:
"Is everybody here on vacation?"

"That kid lives at the lake year-round.
His dad's the rental agent," Crystal says

"Mr. Glaze? My sister walks his dog."
I hold my hand like a visor to my eyes

she points to a boy on a towel
absorbed in a video game
older than us
wearing cut offs
a leather band wraps his wrist

> *hair the color of sand*
> *back curved like the moon*
> *blending into the beach*
> *lonely afternoon*

living at a lake resort
isn't a vacation for everyone.

THE TALE OF
LAKE LUCY

Evie swims over to us
hauls herself aboard the bouncy raft
using the rope ladder:
"I just heard the weirdest thing
from that boy in the blue bathing suit."

"Oh, him,"
Crystal says:
"He doesn't know anything."

Crystal could get on my nerves
without a whole lot of effort:
"What'd he say?"

"It's about how the lake got its name.
Kind of creepy."
Evie dangles her legs over the edge

"I know that story," Crystal says

"Go on, Evie."
wish a hundred horse flies
would pick Crystal up and carry her off

Evie clears her throat:
"Lake Lucy got its name
a long time ago when this girl..."

"Named Lucy, of course,"
Crystal says:
"Tell the story right, if you're going to tell it."

"I'm getting to that."
Evie presses her lips together as if she's cold

"You're too slow."
Crystal shakes her head

"Fine, you tell it."

Blas huffs:
"Will somebody finish?"

two spots flame on Evie's cheeks:
"Lucy got in a rowboat one night."

"Halloween," Crystal says

"He didn't say it was Halloween."

Crystal shifts her gaze around the trampoline:
"I'm pretty sure it was."

I bark:
"What happened?"

everyone on the beach snaps
their heads toward us
Dad's right
sound travels well over water

Evie stares across the lake:
"There was a terrible storm. Lucy got
in her rowboat to row to the other side."
she lowers her voice:
"She disappeared into the fog
and was never seen again."

"Never?"
I frown

Crystal nods at us:
"And they never found the boat either."

"So?" Blas says:
"What's that got to do
with anything?"

"Crystal's eyes widen
like two inflatable inner tubes:
"Haven't you heard about people's towels
and rafts and floaties going missing?"
she flings her arms toward the shore:
"Right off their docks."
she shudders:
"Swallowed by Lake Lucy.
Never to be seen again."

we gaze at the peaceful lake
Evie draws her legs from the rim of the float

sunshine bakes our backs
a white motorboat with a blood red band
surges along the opposite shore
waves strum the sides of the raft

Evie balances on its lip:
"I'm not going to let a dumb ghost story

and careless people losing their stuff
keep me from swimming."
drops like a cannonball into the water

wait for the bubbles to clear
for Evie to pop up.

THE ALMOST
INVITATION

Blas and I hang our heads
over the edge of the raft

his eyes are alarm bells:
"How long can Evie hold her breath?"

lake water is smooth and quiet
my own rippling scared face
stares back at me

"What are you all looking for? A ghost?"
Evie laughs as she clings to the rope ladder
on the other side of the trampoline
paddles back to the slide

"Is she your sister?"
Crystal's hair sticks to her head in strips:
"She's stupid."
slides into the water like a seal
follows Evie

"Hey, only I can insult my sister,"
I yell to Crystal's splashing feet

"Forget about Crystal,"
Blas says:
"I have an RC car. We can share it."

"Race you."
swim my best steady strokes
to the shore

I'm a strong runner
but Blas beats me in swimming
shoots ahead to get his car

year-round boy scowls at him
from behind his game

an offer to join us
dies in my throat.

MR. CRUNCH IS A
PILLOW

Evie comes ashore
uses Mr. Crunch as a pillow
while she reads

yuck
all that sand and water

she's long stopped
talking about Noah

she must not care
what happens to
her favorite stuffed animal either.

HOUSE OF MY DREAMS

Blas sets aside a hydro lacrosse set
we can use in the water:
"We bought these, too."

we move away from people:
"Where'd you get them?"

Blas shows me how the car drives on two wheels:
"Doogie's Dollar Emporium
in Stanley."

"Doogie? What a funny name."

he laughs:
"They have everything. Even a
big pet section. We got a new collar
and toys to bring home to our dog."

he and I take turns
with his remote-control car
no problem spinning on the sand
or churning water on the lake

"When did you get to Lake Lucy?"
he hands me the control
I spin the car three-sixty
before it gets stuck in a hole

Blas hurries to scoop up the car
ticks off his fingers:
"Four days ago. What
about you?"

"Three days. We fished
from the dock yesterday."

"We don't have a dock. Too
steep to the water."

"We're next to
the abandoned house when
you turn off the main road."
house of my dreams
house in my dreams
haven't slept since I found out
we're staying at Lake Lucy

bags under my eyes prove it

Blas sets the car near the water:
"I saw that house. Creepy."

metal mailbox
leans toward the house
a ghost magnet
tugs at me, too
whenever I stand on the driveway

even Dad wonders why a house
in this packed vacation place

has weeds as high as the windows
and looks like it's been abandoned
forever

"When we're outside
sometimes I hear noises
coming from it."

"Really?"

"Faint noises. Maybe not.
Maybe it's the wind in the trees."
I shiver at the thought
of quivering trees
they're afraid of something
only they have seen
and plunge in:
"It looks like it's haunted.
Do you believe in ghosts?"

THE TALKING BLUE
HEAD OF ADVICE

Blas looks beyond me
to Lake Lucy
gently lapping the shore:
"I believe in ghosts, do you?"

"I haven't ruled it out," I say

Blas takes a deep breath
crosses his ankles
eases himself to the damp sand
nods at the space next to him
for me to sit, too

I thump to the ground

he brushes sand off the RC car's
giant wheels:
"My cousin says
she's visited by
a floating blue head."

"A blue head?"
why not a green one

or a pink one?
"When?"

"Mostly at night."

"Where?"
I picture a girl
chased by a glowing blue ball
around her backyard

Blas's arms drift above his head:
"It rises in front of her
when she's in bed."
his arms fall to his side

"Really?"
I study Blas's face
for signs of a smirk
nothing but a squint
because we face the sun:
"Does it talk to her?
Is she scared?"
I swat a horse fly before
it pinches me

"In the beginning
she was afraid,
but now
she's used to it.
She talks about
her problems."
Blas twists his lips
as if sand blew in his mouth:
"Not all ghosts are scary. Some
can be helpful."
he glances over his shoulder
at his family on a quilt:

"My cousin says it's
her mom's best friend
who died
a long time ago."

"And she chose
to come back as a
blue head?"

Blas squeezes a handful
of sand:
"I'm not sure she actually died.
I'm not sure she was ever alive."

bubbles of lake water
swirl over our toes

my mouth is so dry
I could drink the lake:
"How'd that happen? Where'd
the blue head come from?"

Blas breathes in a sail-full of air
and explains:

Blue-Headed Ghost Origin
noun
1. Cheshire Woods
"The blue-headed ghost snuck into the pocket
of a notebook my cousin was carrying while
she wandered around Cheshire Woods where
her mom and my mom grew up, and she carried
it home with her, and no, she didn't tell her mom
about it, only me."

I block the sun with a hand:
"I never knew anyone

who saw a ghost before.
Or talked with one. Or
wrote him a letter."
a letter on paper
not an email
or text
why didn't I think of that before?

a letter means
not having to walk up
to the dilapidated door and ask:
Why are you in my dreams?
What do you want?
When are you going
to leave me alone?

sit up
glance at Evie
swatting horse flies
maybe Evie will put it
in the mailbox for me

Blas grins:
"A letter? Are you thinking
of writing a letter to
whatever lives in the house
next to yours? Count me in!"

GHOST LETTER

I can't wait to leave the
        sandy beach
        warm lake water
        sunshine
        new friend (who believes in ghosts)

        and

        write a LETTER
        to a GHOST!

maybe even drop it in the mailbox

or get Evie to do that.

...Hold On...

Doubt darts like a shadow in my head
a cloud blocking the sun
scum skimming a pond

I can't write a letter to a ghost

(Why not? You've emailed
Grandma
your sixth-grade teacher
and Coach)

if I do
he'll never answer it

(What if he does? Maybe he'll
stop ~~haunting~~ visiting you in your dreams)

I don't know what to write

(Blas has secondhand experience
with a floating blue head. He'll help you)

I won't take it to the house

I won't go any place that's
dark and closed up[2]

(We're talking
paper
pencil
mailbox by the road
not even a stamp)

who are you, anyway, inside-head-voice?
you sound like Evie

(It's a mailbox by the road! You'll never
get any sleep unless you do it.)

---

[2]Dark and Closed Up

No place quite as dark as Grandma's attic   *Dad didn't know I fell asleep*
no one heard me scream as I awoke   *before he shut the pull-down stairs*
when I was three   *I'd hidden in a closet*
I'd hidden in a closet   *when I was three*
before he shut the pull-down stairs   *No one heard me scream as I awoke*
Dad didn't know I fell asleep.   *no place quite as dark as Grandma's attic.*

PEN PALS

I'm about to be pen pals
with a g**h**ost

the only way to
drop the dr**e**ams

ha**l**t the hauntings
nix the nightmares

wil**l** be to write him
pen to paper

boy t**o** ghost.

Rough Draft

Clouds scuttle across the sky
wind stirs dry sand and
ruffles bubbles at the water's edge

Mom and Dad stretch on our blanket
Crystal furiously digs a hole
next to her younger sister

Blas's mom and dad wade into the water
supporting his baby brother

year-round boy balls up his towel
leaves

Blas and I tip our heads closer
the remote-control balances on the car
we lower our voices

"What are we going to write
in the letter?"
Blas says

we? love it

brush sand off my hands:
"We can start with easy questions
like—

How old are you?"

Blas nods:
"What's your name?"

Mr. Crunch wiggles
between us
says in a gruff voice:

"Are you haunting my dreams?"

along the woods
stalks of dried weeds shiver.

MIND LINKS

Evie shakes her stuffed lizard
between me and Blas
giggles

I lean toward her
whisper-shout:
"Were you listening to us?"

Evie fluffs Mr. Crunch's beard:
"No."

"Then why'd you ask if the ghost
is haunting my dreams?"

she shrugs:
"It popped into my head."

maybe our twin brain-bonding thing
finally kicked in because
I never told her about my dreams
Evie throws Mr. Crunch on her towel
runs into the water

Blas's eyes are as dark and deep
as the middle of the lake:
"Your dreams are haunted?"

my throat crackles like dry weeds:
"Yes."

"What's he look like?
What does he say?" Blas asks

I shiver:
"He doesn't say
anything. He's trying to
tell me something. But I
wake up and the whole
thing slips away."

Blas glances at Evie:
"We should talk to my cousin."

THE WARNING

Blas texts his cousin
who tells us to help the ghost
maybe he has a problem?
she won't tell anyone
everyone needs help
occasionally

we make mental notes
about what to say in the letter

I'll text Blas
update him
plan to meet again

and check out the house
look for ghost clues
a detail to add to the note

when my parents drive us home
and pass the dilapidated house
Dad says:

"Keep away from that place.
I don't want to see either of you
going over there."

Evie's Scar

Evie wrinkles her forehead
at Dad's warning

when she wiggles her eyebrows
a tiny scar dances above

her left eye
Dad should ask her

if she wants to use his camera
when she breaks into the haunted house.

Scartastic

Before she leaves the house
to walk Mr. Glaze's dog
Evie whispers:
"I can look in the windows
at the house next door.
For a price."

she didn't get that scar
on her forehead for nothing

unless back-flipping
off the diving board
when she's five

is nothing.

THE BRIBE

On the driveway
facing the tumble-down house
with my baseball glove and ball
the scent of ripe fish
blows across the front yards

feel a tug on my legs
like my fishing line caught a boot
like the house wants me

a cold slimeball
snuffles my fingers

"Help!"
break the house's draw on me
throw my baseball glove in the air
bolt toward our house

my glove thuds on the driveway
spin around at Evie's laugh
wipe my dog nose-smeared hand on my shorts

Evie winds Popcorn's leash in her left hand

sticks out her right hand
nods at the house:
"Candy."

"Gum?"
dig in my pocket for **my** last piece
of Spear-O Mint

Evie examines the wrapper
slides it in her pocket:
"Come on, boy."

she and Popcorn disappear
into the tall grass
as she leads him next door.

A TREE EATS MY SNEAKER

Little white dog hops up and down
by Evie's side as she peers in the windows
of the haunted house

she picks up a stick
shakes it above Popcorn's head
as she leads him to our driveway:
"Here, boy, can you catch this?"

plonk my hands on my hips:
"Well?"

"Well, what?"
a blank look skims her face

"What did you see?"
I reverse my Diamondbacks baseball cap

"Where?"
Evie says

stomach twists:
"The windows."

Evie looks at the eyesore house
then at me:
"It's a mess inside. Looks like
someone left in a hurry."
she and Popcorn zigzag around our driveway

"In a hurry?"
hmmm
"Anything else?"

Popcorn jumps after the stick
Evie giggles:
"I don't think so."

my sneakers crunch on the gravel walkway

"Here's your baseball glove, Jayce."
Evie tosses it high in my direction
when I leap to catch it
it wedges in a tree limb

yank off a sneaker
toss it at the tree
glove falls to the ground
now sneaker's jammed in its branches

Evie laughs
takes a sharp breath:
"That reminds me of something else
that's not in the right place. Those drawings
where you search for things hidden in the picture."

she watches my pogo imitation
under the branch:
"Something in the house
doesn't belong either."

sweat stings my sleepy eyes
yank off my other shoe:
"What?"

Evie lets Popcorn chew on the stick:
"In the middle of the room
is a rowboat."

HOUSE + BOAT = HOUSEBOAT

"A rowboat?"
wind kicks up
rustling the tree
my sneaker falls
whacks me on the head

"Oww."
stagger around
my shoeless feet
find the toothy gravel:
"Oh, oh, ouch."
finish my tree-and-gravel dance
sprawl over a brick border
in the flower bed

Mom calls us to late lunch:
"Jayce, you're not allowed to play
in the flower beds at home. Why do
you think you could play in them here?"

guess I'm too busy thinking about

the rowboat in the ghost house next door!

LUNCH + DINNER = LINNER

I follow Evie
returning Popcorn the dog
to the Glazes' house
at the entrance to the resort
the only house with no lake view

    maybe we'll find out why
    the kid at the lake
    the year-round boy
    his son
    is so angry

    or if he rents many houses
    with boats in their living rooms

the office sticks out
from his house
two parking spaces
roll up to the addition

screen door squeals
as Evie opens it

Mr. Glaze sits at a desk
in front of a curtain
looking through a large
magnifying glass
with giant pincers
and bowls of beads:
"Hi, kiddos."

Mrs. Glaze fills a candy bowl
at the desk

a water cooler crowds
a brochure rack of
caverns
bus schedules
waterfall hikes
golf courses

giant blue empty bottles
stack next to it

nudge Evie
the water dispenser
has a built in
doggie bowl

Evie giggles:
"Hi. We're bringing back
your good boy."

Mrs. Glaze closes the bag:
"Popcorn loves his walks with you."

"He sure does, Vivian."
Mr. Glaze stands
hikes up his shorts:
"Thanks so much, Evie, Jayce.

You're spoiling Popcorn."
plucks a mini chocolate bar:
"Thanks, Vivian, my dear.
Don't mind if I do."
chuckles and offers the bowl to us

the real reason Evie
walks Popcorn

Evie takes a handful
I find a stick of Spear-O Mint gum
Mrs. Glaze fades into the curtain

Mr. Glaze walks
around his desk
trades the leash for
an elastic beaded bracelet:
"Here's a little
something special
for you. I make jewelry
in my spare time."

Evie squeals
Popcorn hops
year-round boy
appears from a split in the curtain.

ANOTHER WARNING

Mr. Glaze:
"Austin, come meet Evie
and Jayce. Their family's renting
next to the Madera place."

Austin folds his arms
uneasy, wiry wearing a
steely gray
t-shirt, its color reflected
in his wild silver eyes
not a friend:
"The Madera's house
is haunted. Stay away from it."

HOW LAKE LUCY
REALLY GOT ITS NAME

Evie chuckles:
"The house next door is haunted?"

I lift my cap
reach for my head
make sure my hair isn't on end

instead of laying on a beach towel
Austin's vertical
he's two years taller than me
that translates to five inches

Mr. Glaze claps a hand
on Austin's shoulder:
"Don't go spreading ghost stories.
No one's lived there for years."

Austin helps himself
to a handful of candy:
"Don't you wonder why nobody
ever rents it?"

I glance at Popcorn lapping

from the bowl attached to the water cooler:
"It's kind of a wreck. Thanks for the gum.
Gotta go."
pluck Evie's elbow

Evie glows at her new bracelet:
"We heard a story about how the lake
got its name."

Mr. Glaze picks up Popcorn:
"That old urban legend isn't true.
In the nineteen-seventies, the man
who built the resort and dug the lake
named it after his daughter. She raised
Maltese pups, like little Popcorn here."

tongue lolls from dog's mouth

I lick my own dry lips:
"What happened to the daughter?"

Mr. Glaze glances at his son:
"Umm, Lucy Madera moved out
in twenty-oh-eight, or so."

"Why didn't she sell it?"
Evie asks

Who cares? Who would want a creeped-out house?

"No one wants to work in it,"
Austin says

Mr. Glaze laughs:
"It's hard getting workers nowadays."

already composing a text in my head

for Blas about Austin and Lucy Madera
push Evie toward the door:
"That's interesting. Thanks for the candy.
Good-bye."

Evie grins at them
shakes her wrist:
"I love the bracelet, Mr. Glaze.
See you later, Austin."

not if I can help it.

LATE AFTERNOON

Evie and I rock in two fishnet swings
hanging under the tall deck
behind the house

repeat Evie's words
letting them knock around my brain
like loose pinballs:
"There's a rowboat
in the middle of the room
in the house next door."

"Yep."
Evie says

"How big is this rowboat?"

chains from the swings squawk
like a phantom parrot
as we swing

"Hard to tell."
she says

pretend to hold a basketball:
"This big?"

maybe it's a boat picture
or as small as a bowl
of fruit on a table

Evie snorts:
"Much bigger than that."

"Bigger than Mr. Crunch?"
Evie's stuffed blue lizard
measures two feet
not counting his foot long tail

she nods

"Like a canoe?"

"Kind of."

a speedboat whirrs by
"Bigger than that?"

she shakes her head:
"It's in pieces. But I
can tell it's a rowboat."

"Weird."
the back of my neck tingles

Maybe:
A ghost needs a boat
because he can't float.

LUCY'S HOUSE

I rotate my swing to glimpse the house
next door through the bushes
toxic-looking weeds grow
between its windows
screens balloon from its back porch
my feet itch to creep through the yard

but

that'll never happen
I can't risk getting too close
I'll get sucked inside

the outside of Lucy's house
is a perfect copy
of the house in my dreams

I bet the inside is a combination
of Grandma's attic
and the scary dream house:

Knee deep in weeds
by a broken mailbox

crossing the threshold
into a twilight room
walls slant toward me
I drown in the murk
of lightlessness

can't see my hands
in front of my face
can't find the door
built into the floor

the ghost doesn't speak
it plucks at my hair
my clothes
my breath
I don't know where
it is or what it wants.

TIME TO GET PROOF

My snoring wakes me. Eleven-forty-three PM. I click off the alarm, turn off the nightlight, make sure my door's closed, and crouch by the window. The windows in the creepy house are black and empty. My legs cramp. I get a folded footstool, hanging on nails in the kitchen, and sit on it in front of the window.

My eyelids drift shut. I knock my chin on the windowsill. That wake-up call's good for fifteen minutes. I decide to set my alarm and try again at three AM.

When the alarm buzzes, I slap the clock to turn it off. Get a drink of water and sit by my window. My breath puffs twin circles of steam on the glass pane. I draw a smiley face in one, and it fades. I huff at the window, and it shows up again.

While I'm busy making a train of faces on the glass, a double set of lights flash from the window next door. They leap to the other window and disappear.

Dad's Digital Camera

My heart and hands flutter
as I fumble in the kitchen
for the camera
in front of the toaster

I'm right

there's a ghost next door

he's dashing through the house
with a pair of lanterns
like the kind we use for camping

can't wait to tell Evie

if nothing more happens on this watch
if I don't get a picture to prove it
Evie won't believe me
I'll lose my best partner

my bravest

I can write a letter to a ghost
I'm not sure I can stick it
in his mailbox.

SECOND WATCH

I settle into a dreamless sleep
until five o'clock slides into home plate
jolting me awake
take my post on the hard seat
by the window

grayish mist lifts from the lake
crawls over the beat-up dock
fingers the weeds,
blue tarp slung over sawhorses,
splintered bench facing the lake

a pair of lights sparks
in one window of the house
moves to the other

lose my balance
slide off the stool
Come on, Jayce. Your chances
of proving a ghost is next door
are slipping away.

MAGICAL MEMORY

I wait two minutes
center the windows next door
in the viewfinder
camera drops from my sweaty hands
thuds on the floor

way to go

hold the camera
to my beating chest
stop breathing
listen if Dad
thunders down the hall—

he'll kill me
if he knows I have his camera
wrench me back from the dead
kill me again
if I break it

shaky feeling flutters
under the bone
in the middle of my chest

inhale until the room stops spinning

silence

turn back to my window
in time to squeeze
the record button

my mind is swished
smooth and level
like the lakeshore

fingers take over
as the ghost flies
from one window
to the next

he's running in circles
in a spiritual ritual
it's all on the magic memory card.

EVIDENCE

No way am I going back to sleep now
watch the clip fifty million times
waiting for Evie to wake up

Evie pokes me in the arm:
"Why are you sleeping with Dad's camera?"

blink at her
rub the crease the camera made in my arm:
"Evie, Austin is right about the ghost next door.
I have proof."
jiggle the camera under her nose

"Let's see."
she holds out her hand:
"Why didn't you use your cell phone?"

drop the camera in her lap:
"It's way too slow. Doesn't respond
right away."

Evie tilts her head
eyes flick over the tiny screen

on the back

my body is ready to crack-crunch
waiting for her face to change into
horror
surprise
anything

either she's used to seeing ghosts
or doesn't care.

PICTURE PROOF HAIKU

Precious camera
evidence of ghostly deeds
batteries are dead.

MEANWHILE...

...the camera recharges itself in the kitchen

    behind boxes of crackers

    I text Blas and update him
    he's waiting for it...

    responds:
    a hundred ghost emojis
    "COOL!"
    a hundred ghost emojis
    "I googled 'Lucy Madera Lake Lucy Stanley Virginia'."

    "Great idea!!!! And??????????????"

    swimming emoji
    "Howard Madera dredged a lake
    from a bunch of sports fields to make a resort
    in nineteen seventy-four and named the lake after his daughter."
    shrugging emoji

    sports fields?
    where would they play baseball?

"Good work!! We'll keep you posted!!"
thumbs up emoji
fireworks emojis
that's for July Fourth
one of my favorite holidays
and to celebrate my independence
from haunted dreams.

Evie's Theory

Evie meets me at the swings under the deck

I tuck an old notebook beneath the cushion:
I'm ready to write him a letter.

Evie whirls in the swing:
"The ghost might be a 'she.' Remember
the story about Lucy? She got in
her rowboat and was never seen again."

hook my fingers in the netting
draw my legs to my chest
my words spiral around me:
"Do you think it's Lucy? Mr. Glaze said she
moved out. Austin didn't say who the ghost
was. It could be Lucy's dad. Or her twin brother."

Evie hoots:
"Twin brother? Ask her if her dad haunted her because
he didn't like dogs, so she tried to row away
and drowned. If you write the letter,
I'll stick it in the mailbox."

calculate my candy stash

Evie climbs the net of the swing like a sailor:
"Is the rowboat in your dreams?"

invisible horse flies crawl over me
throat tightens I swallow a lump of air:
"It's so dark, I bump into everything. I
can't tell if it's furniture or a boat. Then
I'm surrounded by something cold and slimy."

she jumps to the ground:
"That must be the ghost."

I jam my toe in the dirt to stop spinning:
"What does she want with me?"

Evie stares beyond the dock to the lake:
"Don't worry. Things aren't always what they seem."

but sometimes they are.

DEAR MR. OR MS. GHOST

I pull out my battered notebook
grip the pen

a motorboat buzzes by
waves slosh under the dock
suck on the pole-like pilings
underneath it
the scent of slimy greenness
wafts up on hot air

bend over the page
remembering questions Blas and I
thought up

better start with easy ones
leave Evie's suggestion about Lucy's
crazed dog-hating dad out for now

my pen drops blobs of blue ink on the page:

Dear Ghost,
I (Jayce) saw you last night running
through your living room with something
like two lanterns or flashlights. Who are
you? I told my sister, Evie. We promise we
won't tell.

Here are some more questions
How old are you?
What is your name?
Why is there a boat in the house?
Are you in my dreams?

Leave your answers in your mailbox.

Your friends,
Jayce, Evie, and Blas (friend)

ON YOUR MARK...

Evie leaves by the time
I finish the letter to the ghost

I fold it into its own envelope
stick it in my pocket

she's in front of the house
sprawled on a blanket
filling in the lines in her *Amazing Fantastical Animals*
stress reducing coloring book
under the tree
I played catch with yesterday

I drop the envelope
in the groove of her book

Evie glances at the folded letter
flips it like a paper football:
"You forgot to tell who it's for."

humph:
"Give me a pencil."

"Gel pen."

"All right. Give me a gel pen."

"What color?"
she says

"Doesn't matter. Just give me one."
acids in my stomach
churn my breakfast into liquid lava

Evie sorts through her pile
I drop to my knees
pick out a black gel pen:
To the Ghost.

"Go ahead."
hand the note to her:
"I'll wait here and watch you."

Evie turns her animal stress reducing coloring book
over to mark her page
neatens her pile of pens
shakes out her hair
smooths it into place

by the time she skips
across the driveway
cutting through both side yards
I'm sure my stomach acids
are burning a hole through my
Big Foot for President T-shirt

Evie stands in front of the mailbox
its door hangs on by a screw

she waves the letter

grins
this is all a joke to her

raise my arm in a
thanks-its-about-time salute
wind gusts
like it thinks I'm signaling
a race
blows so hard
pages of seahorses
monkey heads
and cobras flicker

stomp to keep them
from blowing away

Evie speeds past me
shrieking her head off
disappears into the house.

...Get Set...

Evie huddles on her bed
with Mr. Crunch

"What happened?"

she laughs in a sickly way:
"That was weird. I was about to put the letter
in the mailbox when the wind blew it from
my hand. Almost as if the ghost
grabbed it from me."
laughs again
shakes her head:
"Of course, that didn't happen."

"Where's the letter now?"

she shrugs:
"I don't know. It cartwheeled
down the road and must be gone by now."

groan:
"If I write another one,
will you deliver it?"

Evie fiddles with her *DeathDrop Tower* T-shirt
from Plummet Park
where Noah won Mr. Crunch for her
smoothing it over her candy-filled belly:
"Ahhhhhhh... Sure."
blink

no time for hesitation
one of us is the brains—me
one of us is the braver—her
this is what it means to be twins
together we're some sort of a super kid

go back to my room
rewrite the letter
add: *P.S. Thanks.*
figure we can't be too polite.

... Go!

Evie hurries off next door
throws the folded note in the mailbox
scoops up pebbles
arranges them inside
skips home

"I made sure it's in the back
of the box so it won't get
blown away since the door doesn't close.
Want to color?"

no
but
she did risk her life:
"Okay."
get my Diamondbacks
baseball cap

we spread out on the quilt
a pile of gel pens between us
raise my head every few minutes
to stare at the mailbox

my left foot vibrates
waiting is not for the impatient:
"We should've given him
something to write with.
How many ghosts carry a pen?"

"You're not going to give him one of mine,"
Evie scoops the gel pens under her arm
like a hen with her chicks

"I'll get something else."
hurry into the house
bring out a stubby pencil

she groans
rushes to stick the pencil in the mailbox:
"The letter's gone."
she plops back on the quilt

shiver:
"What?"

Evie throws her head back and laughs:
"Got you."

"Very funny."
I pick a cobra picture
closest thing to a diamondback
add more black
to the cobra's hood

a spot drops on my page:
"Look at this."
swing the book around to show Evie
specks splatter my page

the sky darkens

raindrops plunk down
Evie screams
rushes into the house

I pull up the corners of the quilt
into a bundle
run after her
throw it in the kitchen

"Thanks for saving my book and pens."
Evie kneels on the floor
scoops them into a bucket

"Sure."
I wonder how someone who dives backwards
off the high dive could be afraid of a little rain
she never was before coming to Lake Lucy

at least I'm afraid of something sensible
like ghosts and nightmares.

Waiting Is Not for The Impatient

The rain is a pain
I shouldn't complain

there're books to be read
while curled on my bed

and Boggle to win
when playing my twin

but ghosts have the time
and haunting's a crime

Please answer my note
about your weird boat.

A Trip Around Lake Lucy

Mom and Dad drive us around the lake
beyond the high school to the small town of Stanley

we pass the post office
and grungy bus depot

park at Stop 'n' Shop
near the tomato-y smells of Paolini's Pizza Palace

Mom pops into the grocery store
Dad picks up an uncooked pizza to bake later

on the other side of the grocery store
ladies enter Hair Quality Salon

we spy our dock through the trees
next to Doogie's Dollar Emporium

and choose something cool at Scooter's Scoop Shop
but more exciting than a double dip of

vanilla ice cream is arriving home to discover
the red flag is up on the mailbox next door!

Like Sitting on an Ant Hill

The rear-view mirror
frames Mom's frowning eyes
she flies past the ghost's house:
"You two will stay indoors
the rest of today."

except for Evie
taking a short trip
to the mailbox:
"I can't. I don't like
when rain plops on my head.
Like a bird,
if you know what I mean."

inside the house
lights flicker
Dad sets out
flashlights and candles

thunder cracks
rain gushes
like the lake

is pouring itself
over the roof

no amount of Boggle
passes the time.

THE RAIN ABSTAINS OR
IT POURS NO MORE

I stand inside the open front door
waiting for Evie
air smells like the lake

she pushes down the red flag
shows me a rock used as a weight
tucks the letter in her pocket
jumps puddles to the house

    follow her inside
    toes tingling
    fingers itching to open
    the ghost's reply.

THE BIG REVEAL

Evie hands me the note:
"Where are we going to read it?"

"Come in my room," I whisper
wipe my hands on my shorts
someone opened and refolded it

Evie giggles as I smooth the paper
on the bedspread
pencil marks are scratched
next to the questions

"He answered them." I gulp

she scoots around to face it:
"Let me see."

we hover over the letter
read it aloud
stopping after each wobbly answer
to see whose eyeballs
pop out of their sockets first:

Dear Ghost,
I (Jayce) saw you last night running
through your living room with something
like two lanterns or flashlights. Who are
you? I told my sister, Evie. We promise we
won't tell.

Here are some more questions
How old are you? 'AS OLD AS THE LAKE'
What is your name? 'CALL ME GHOST FOR NOW'
Why is there a boat in the house? 'I CAN'T
Are you in my dreams? 'SURE'   SWIM'

Leave your answers in your mailbox.

Your friends,
Jayce, Evie, and Blas (friend)

an icy shiver rips down my spine:
"I'm right. There *is* a ghost."

Evie claps:
"Good job, Jayce. Do we tell
Mom and Dad?"

I frown:
"I don't think they'd like it.
Especially Mom. Or else,
they'll say we made it all up."

pull out the notebook hidden
under some T-shirts in a drawer
"I'm going to write another letter."

Dear Ghost,

We got your letter. Do you remember me? I'm the kid who asked you all those questions. Well, I have more.

Are you a boy or a girl?

Can you read my handwriting?

Is this too much questions for you?

Are you small or big?

Is that your rowboat in the living room?

                              Your friends,

                    Jayce, Evie, and Blas

LETTER NUMBER TEW
TEW TEW

I fold the new letter into its own envelope
using my thumbnail to crease it

tuck the returned letter in a pocket
on the back cover of the notebook

wait in the doorway
as cardinals call to each other:

tew tew tew
time to update Blas

Evie crosses the wet grass
trudges to the driveway

"Come on," she says
"They have old movies here. It's your turn
to do something I want to do."

the price I pay
for my burden of fear.

DREAM LETTER

A voice on the TV screen warbles,
"Someday my prince will come."
That's right, lady. Keep waiting.
Watching and waiting.

my eyes roll around their sockets
as if they don't fit
so sleepy
must be that late night
me watching for a ghost
and the ghost watching me
in my dreams

my head nods lower

                    lower

until it rests on my chest
a new dream blooms in my head:

"Come closer, Jayce," a voice
calls to me over the lake
a clear see-through kind of voice

from the dock behind the scary house
a muttering
mummering
babbling
buzzing
string of sound like
someone (thing)
threw out a fishing line
of groans and squawks
hooking me
drawing me toward it

"Who are you?"
I stand on our dock
"What do you want?"

boats rest on top of dense cold mist
swirling on the water
I test if the mist will hold me
walk across to
the beat-up dock next door
like walking on fresh snow

step onto the ghost's dock
boards are missing
drop to my hands and knees
peer into the empty space
no water
only mist
thick and rumbly
like a cloud before it rains

the old mailbox sticks up on the dock
flag pointing like a red finger
the open door swings back and forth
on its single hinge

a letter inside the mailbox
under a rock
addressed to: J

I reach for it—
Where's Evie? Why isn't
she doing this?

"Read it. Heed it," scrapes the voice
from the back of the mailbox
a frosty hand with long red nails
pushes the letter
the rock
one final shove

they explode from the mailbox
dump on my toe.

Magic Mirror Eyes

I don't know if it's the sight of
the ghost's hand that wakes me
or the metal bowl hitting my foot
popcorn is everywhere

my heart churns faster than
the propeller on a speedboat
I gasp for breath

Evie faces me
eyes like two of the evil Queen's
Magic Mirrors in *Snow White*
big and empty with scariness
carved into the edges

"What's wrong with you?"
she says in a funny way
like popcorn is stuck in her throat

"Remember I asked the ghost
if he could be in my dreams? And he said yes?"
I wipe sweat from my lip

Evie's head bobs
her eyebrows reach for each other
filling in the space above her nose

"I fell asleep and really saw him. It wasn't a feeling.
I saw his hand. And I know it's him."

Evie sips her iced tea
eyebrows relax to their normal positions:
"I'm starting to believe you."
points to the floor:
"You better clean that up before Mom sees it."
she punches the volume button higher

scoop the popcorn into my bowl
sweep the rest under the couch
wander into the kitchen

the letter in my dream
so close
if I could only read it.

ALL CHARGED UP

The digital camera
lays on a cushion of paper napkins

I whip the cord from the wall socket
find the video of the ghost
running through Lucy's house

dangle the camera by its strap
in Evie's face

"What are those lights?"

"Flashlights or lanterns."

she plays it over:
"They're moving."

"Like he's running through the living room."

"Or flying."
she looks at me with Magic Mirror eyes:
"I think we should tell Dad."

"He'll say it's my imagination. I'll never
get to figure it out. We won't be allowed
to keep writing the ghost."
I'll be haunted forever

wrap the strap around the camera
set it on a table on top of magazines:
"Why don't we check the mailbox now?"

"It hasn't been long enough."

by the time we finish arguing
it's dark outside.

THE EVENING
ISN'T EVEN

Huge trees
brush against the sky
wiping away sunlight

no streetlights
no equal light and dark
no balance
no edges to keep the dark
from bleeding into the light

it's vacationing in a box
and someone dropped a lid·on it
suffocating me

no checking the mailbox's flag
till morning.

THE LONG AND WINDING WIND

The next day the lake glitters
like a thousand diamonds

I stand by the open front door
my spy glasses target
the clump of tall weeds
hiding the mailbox
if they shift a little
I'll see the flag
run my tongue on my dry lips

no wind
long wait
need to
hydrate

"What're you up to, buddy?"
Dad's voice makes me flinch

"Looking for wildlife."
truth

"Use those binoculars

to look at the lake. You might
see jumping fish."
Dad sips coffee from his mug:
"We'll go fishing in a while."

"Good idea."
turn back to the open door

rain plops from my dancing tree partner
to the puddles
wind sends a spray of water

rub the glass eye pieces dry
on my T-shirt
wind gusts again
wild grass in front of the mailbox
parts like a curtain

red flag points to the sky.

No Time to Give Up

My socks slide on the floor
as I round the corner in the hallway
dash downstairs
to the cool musty basement

along the back wall
streaky windows look like someone
washed them with milk

fishing poles clatter to the floor
now is a good time for Evie to leave

"Sorry, Dad," she says

wave to her
point to the ceiling
we rush upstairs to my room

I dive in my backpack for a bag of chips:
"The red flag is up."

Evie examines the 'best by' date:
"You're coming, too."

Evie takes her time
picking her way to the mailbox
her shoulders rise as she takes a breath
before sticking her hand in the opening

throws the rock on the ground
plucks the letter out of the opening
runs stiff-legged back to me
tosses me the damp letter

I smooth the paper on my bed
hold my breath as we read the scrawl:

Dear Ghost,

We got your letter. Do you remember

me? I'm the kid who asked you all those

questions. Well, I have more.

Are you a boy or a girl? 'NEITHER'

Can you read my handwriting? 'KIND OF'

Is this too much questions for you? 'MAYBE'

Are you small or big? 'DEPENDS'

Is that your rowboat in the living room?
'CAN'T SAY'   Your friends,

                    Jayce, Evie, and Blas

"'Can't say'? Why not?"

I want to know if the ghost is the real Lucy

the one the lake claimed on Halloween all those years ago
and took her name

"He wrote something else."
Evie points to the bottom
of the note:
"'don't ask about the boat anymore.'
He sure is a grumpy ghost."
she laughs like a sick hyena

stare at her for a second
I don't know who's scarier
Evie or the ghost
rip off another sheet from my notebook

"What are you doing?"

"I'm going to ask him why
he doesn't want to talk about the boat."

"Jayce, that's dumb."
she slides off the bed
pulls the bag of chips apart:
"Give up."

no!
text Blas
update him
he's as excited as me:
Go for it!!!!
we have blue-ghost-head-confidence

"Give up? Why? Watch this."
scribble another letter.

Dear Ghost,

What's your real name? I can't keep calling you ghost.

Besides maybe you're not for real. You were in one of my dreams.

What was my dream about?

Does the name Lucy mean anything to you?

Why do you have a boat in your living room?

Fill in the blank. My name is_____.

Your friends,

Jayce, Evie, and Blas

Playing Catch (With) the Ghost

I hand the creased paper to Evie
she munches the last of the chips
wipes her hands on her shorts
folds her arms in a sort of hug

take that as a no
thrust my arm into my backpack
searching for bribery material
fingers wedge in a gooey gritty mess

brain flash:
"I'll give you my dessert tonight,
if you deliver this."

"Okay."
she tucks the note in her pocket

That was easy. She must know
we're not having fruit for dessert.

follow her
trying to scrape out the grossness
under all my nails

on the front step
Dad and guilty looking Evie
stand on the driveway

"We're going to play catch,"
she says loudly even for her
she licks her lips

grab my glove and ball
from inside the door

Dad points:
"Stay away from that house."

Evie swivels:
"That old broken-down thing?"

"It looks like someone's been
snooping around over there."
he nods at the flattened path of grass

"Catch, Evie."
throw the ball to her

she misses it
right on cue
chases the ball
into the flat grass path

wait for Dad to close the front door
Evie pushes down the flag
plants the rock on the note

curtain in the living room parts
Dad's face hovers in the window.

Time for a Jayce
Strategy

baseball ploy
double fake

stand at home
switch to bunt

wind up hitting
ball like normal

hope my fake
fakes Dad out.

THE FAKE THAT
ISN'T FAKE

Dad grinds the gravel under his sandals:
"What did I tell you about going next door?
You don't know who or what's living there.
We didn't know we rented a house next to—"

impact position:
"Dad, it's okay. No one lives next door."
bunt position:
"Except a ghost!"

Dad scowls from me
to the broken house:
"A ghost. Right."

switch to impact position:
"We write him letters. And he answers us!"
slap my thigh and laugh
Outta the park!

Dad shifts his gaze from me to Evie

she whacks the ball into my stomach
as she passes me:

"Let's watch a movie."

Dad glances at me as I follow them:
"A ghost? Good one, Jayce. Stay on this side
of the property. It's too nice for you both
to spend the rest of your vacation inside."

Evie bunches her lips together
death rays shoot from her eyes

rub my mouth to hide a smile
Dad doesn't suspect my fake is
a fake.

A Mess at the Public Beach

Instead of a movie
Mom packs a picnic lunch
text Blas about meeting at the lake

eat as soon as we get to the beach
Evie uses Mr. Crunch as a table
balancing her paper plate on his back

Crystal and her sister carve holes
out of the sand and bury toys

I wander toward trees circling the beach
waiting for lunch to digest

wishing we bought an RC car
at Doogie's Dollar Emporium

> *"Hey, dude, get out of there."*
> *Austin glares at me from a towel*

> *bonk my head on a low branch*
> *"I'm not doing anything wrong,"*

"Nobody's supposed to be in the woods."

"Why not? They don't belong to you."

*"These woods are protected. It's an
environmental thing. You wouldn't
understand."*

"Jayce," Blas calls

take off past the year-round boy
not before he trips me
get a mouth full of sand
lose my Diamondbacks baseball cap
spit and give the kid my best angry face

    since he's bigger than me

lope towards Blas
so Austin doesn't think I'm
trying to get away from him
when I am
wonder if the year-round kid
is a year-round mess.

The Recap with No Cap

Blas and I swim to the slide float
bounce on the bouncy float

I sum up the ghost's answers
to our letters
add the video evidence

Blas's mouth gapes as dark
as the empty mailbox

wait for a tiny white hand
with teensy red nails to dart out
poke me in the eye

"Take me to the house
so I can see the rowboat for myself."
Blas jerks his thumb toward his family:
"My parents won't care. How about
if I go home with you today?"

if Blas comes back with me
I'll be forced to go to the house
with him

glance at Blas's arms to check
if he's strong enough to yank
me out of the house
if I get sucked into it:

"I'll get in big trouble with my dad
if I go over there." *think fast and bluff*
"But maybe we can work something out."

Blas's face lights up
like a ghost's lantern.

A Visit from Blas

I show Blas the ghost's lantern video
he watches it five times
shaking his head:
"You'd think he'd get dizzy but,
I guess he is a ghost."

we take two fishing poles to our dock
sit on the edge
an excuse to get a look at the house next door
bait hooks with balls of bread
drop the lines into the lake

Blas tips his head:
"The ghost house looks worse up close."

waves slurp the giant telephone pole-like
pilings holding up the dock next door

the back of the empty house is hidden
by barbed briars and horrible hedges

"Nice, huh?"
our red and white fishing bobbers

bobble on the water:
"Do you hear something?"

"Sounds like tapping."
Blas twists around
jerks his thumb at the house next door:
"I think it's coming from over there."

BLAS TAKES A PEEK

My mind zips around
if everything works out
Blas can go next door
report everything back to me
while I keep watch:
"You want to have a look?"

"What about your dad?"
Blas says

"He's probably taking a nap. But if
he catches us, I'll be in so much trouble."

tap
tap
bang

"There it goes again. I have an idea."
hand Blas my pole
drag over two webbed chairs
balance the rods behind them

we run up the steps toward the house

crouch under the deck

"Your sister won't tell if she sees us, will she?"
Blas asks

"She's in on it, too. I'll keep watch here
while you have a look in the window.
Use the one closest to the lake. Just in case."

thumbs up

"I'll warn you with this whistle."
cup my hands together
blow into the mouthpiece
my bent thumbs make
sounds like a foghorn

Blas wiggles through the high grass
to the side of the abandoned house
stoops under the window ledge
head pops up

a dog yelps in the distance
maybe from the other side of the lake
sound travels far over water Dad tells
me and Evie so we won't yell

Blas draws his head into his shoulders
turtle-style

give him the thumbs up sign

he balances his fingertips against the rotting wood

yapping dog sounds louder
and louder
unless the dog is on a boat

... wait a minute
that's Mr. Glaze's dog

clasp my hands together and blow
nothing comes out
cup my hands wider
smaller
no foghorn
not even a toot

lick my lips
shift my hands
until I coax a hoarse sound
from my hands

Blas turns around

I wave him in

he snakes through the tall grass

we dive through the bushes
land at Dad's feet

"Hi, boys. What are you up to?"

THE REPORT

I brush off my shorts:
"Mr. Glaze is coming over with his dog."

"I'll get Evie. She loves that little mutt."
Dad disappears into the basement

Blas and I hurry to the dock
flop in the chairs
breathing hard

"That was close."
Blas glances behind us
reels in his empty fishhook

I hand him the bread bag:
"What'd you find?"

"It's like looking underwater. Then
I saw the rowboat. Talk about weird."
Blas reaches inside the bag.
"How many people put a boat in their living room?
And not even a whole one."
he tacks another blob of bread on the hook

I pinch part of a slice and roll it into a ball:
"We're not talking about people here."
brush breadcrumbs off my lap
hands shaking so much I'm
afraid I'll stab myself baiting the hook:
"Anything else?"

     he lays his pole across his knees
     a buzz hums in the distance

I search for a horse fly on the loose

I can tell Blas is trying to squeeze
the image of the boat
to the front of his brain:
"Something long and shiny is by the boat."

     a sword
     a saber
     a scimitar?

A Very Handy Ghost
with Problems

The motorboat with the red band zips by
Blas follows it with his eyes:
"A hammer was next to the boat."

my eyebrows hit the clouds:
"Are you sure? That explains the tapping noise."

Blas claps his knee:
"Yes! 'Cause there were nails next to it.
I thought they were tiny pencils, like the
kind you use for miniature golf."

"Why would a ghost need a hammer?"

"He's a ghost, not a magician."
Blas says:
"He'd have to use a hammer to build something."

"Or fix something. Like a boat."
take off my backup Yankees baseball cap
swipe the sweat from my forehead

"That boat is beyond repair."

"But if he flies, why would he need a boat?"
I replace my hat

Blas casts his line in the lake:
"Unless he doesn't know he's dead."

I didn't count on a ghost with problems.

Low Tide Can't Hide Ghosts on the Underside

Blas tugs on his fishing line:
"I wonder who lived there
before it was abandoned."

"Mr. Glaze said it was Lucy."
the sudden chill that wraps its fingers
around me reaches for Blas

"For real?"
he shudders
makes that mailbox mouth again

"Could the ghost really be Lucy?"
train my eyes on the house next door

"In the letter, didn't he, or she, say she was
'as old as the lake'?"

"Yeah."
shudder despite the sun blazing on my back
a weird feeling replaces the chill
we're being watched
overheard

spied on

tide is low
a raft can fit under the dock
I meander over the decking
checking the spaces between the slats of wood

"What's up?"
Blas asks

"Just having a look."
clouds cover the sun
a cool breeze puffs across the lake

Blas stands and knocks over his chair:
"Look behind you."

my feet freeze
like I'm standing on
an air-conditioning vent.

The Wandering Ghost

Mist rises between the boards
cold and clammy
curls and stretches toward us before disappearing

"Let's get outta here,"
I say to Blas's back
we sprint up the steps to the deck
outside the kitchen

catch our breath
as we lean over the railing

"I-I had a dream that happened."
jiggle my head like I have fleas
this is all wrong
the ghost is next door
Lucy is next door
it's too scary to think
he—
she
wanders around

Blas's eyes darken

and shine until I see my tiny scared self
reflected in them

"Ghosts don't come out during the day."
when did I become such a know-it-all on ghosts?
"Seriously, it was Evie under the dock in a raft."

"Evie? And the mist?"

"Light a match and blow it out."
I strike an imaginary match
of course smoke isn't cold
which was what that mist was
"Smoke rises between the boards.
I'll remember that little prank."

"Right, right."
Blas nods
jerks his thumb toward the screen door
where Evie sits sketching at the kitchen table:
"Then who's that?"

CRUNCH CRUNCH CRUNCH

That night I jolt awake from the scream
of a thousand sirens

on the dresser
my catcher's mitt quakes
the baseball rolls off
thuds on the floor
as my parents
pound down the hall

I creep past the bathroom
peek in Evie's room

Mom holds Evie around the shoulders
Dad opens all her dresser drawers
the closet
peers under her bed:
"I'll check the car."
he brushes past

Evie turns to me:
"Mr. Crunch is gone. Somebody
stole him. I've looked everywhere."

step into the room:
"When did you see him last?"

Evie glances at the window:
"I took him to the beach. Do you
think Blas took him?"

"No way."
not his nature
unless he learned to miniaturize Mr. Crunch
and put him in his pocket

Dad returns:
"Not in the car. We'll check
the public beach tomorrow."

I step on the deck outside the kitchen
lean on the railing
the boards are warm under my feet
from the sun that day

the sky looks like torn blue jeans
dark with a line of shredded clouds
the hills chomp back at the sky
red stains the peaks like blood

If Crystal can bury her little sister
in the sand, she can do other
mean things.

as I fall asleep
crickets under my window shriek:
crunch
crunch
crunch

SETTING A DEADLINE

The next morning
my heart pounds me out of sleep
I lay still
eyes closed
try to remember my dream:

dashing upstairs and downstairs
always looking for I-don't-know-what

the dream slips away

when I open my eyes
Evie's hollow-eyed face hovers over me
she dangles my spy glasses above my head

"What are you doing? You look terrible.
Did you sleep last night?"

her eyes have that dark raccoon look to them
"I borrowed these. The flag is up.
Get the letter."

I sit up:

"Why don't you get it?"

"I can't anymore. Everything is bad
since Mr. Crunch is missing. Dad went
to the beach early this morning
and couldn't find him."
she lowers the binoculars to my chest

one lost lizard
and Evie's nerve is gone

"Dad's playing golf with Mr. Glaze
and Austin. Go."

Mom sets up the Scrabble board on the deck:
"Grab a muffin and orange juice. Come outside
and play with us."

"I'll be there in ten minutes."
I work best under pressure.

THE PITCH

Spend the next six minutes
pacing the driveway
fighting the pull on my legs
drawing me to the vine-choked door

hurry back to my room
get my ball and glove
if I throw the baseball at the mailbox
I'll want to get it back
that'll force me to get the letter

on the driveway
line up my shoulder with home plate
that is, the mailbox
nod to invisible catcher
fast pitch it is
wind up
snap ball off wrist
whack

direct hit to the mailbox
its door twists off its hinge
drops

clanks on rocks on the ground

dash over
scoop up my baseball
snatch the letter

can't tell if runner is
safe or out at home.

A Nice Warm Ice Bath
Before Scrabble

Rush into the house
scared I can't understand the letter
realize it's upside down

"Coming, Jayce?"
Mom calls from the porch

"Be right there."
blink
focus on the words
turn the page around:

Dear Ghost,

What's your real name? I can't keep

calling you ghost.

Besides maybe you're not for real. You

were in one of my dreams.

What was my dream about? 'I SCARED YOU'

Does the name Lucy mean anything to

you? 'IT'S THE NAME OF THE LAKE. DON'T YOU
KNOW WHERE YOU ARE'

Why do you have a boat in your living

room? 'I USE IT TO FISH HA HA'

Fill in the blank. My name is GHOST.

                    Your friends,

            Jayce, Evie, and Blas

she scrawled a P.S. at the bottom

feel like I'm dipped in ice water

at the same time my blood freezes

numb
I sit on the end of my bed
unable to move

Evie pops in the doorway:
"Did you get the letter?
Show me. Mom's waiting."

I bite my lip
not noticing the pain.

A Peculiar Plea

I crease the letter
stick it in my pocket:
"I'll show you later."

Evie holds her hand out:
"Why?"

"Same old stuff. Don't worry
about it. Hurry."
flap my hands so she'll leave

Evie trots off
I unfold the letter
reread it to be sure I understand

what she wrote
at the bottom of the page.

SHE DOESN'T EXACTLY WRITE THIS BUT THIS IS WHAT MY SCRABBLE-ADDLED BRAIN SEES:

```
. . . . . L . . .
. . . . . I S . .
. . . . . Z . . .
. . . . . A . . .
. . . F . R . . .
. . C O R D S . .
. . . O . . . . .
. L . T O A S T .
. E . . . . I . .
M A I L B O X . .
. V . . U . . . .
T H E . N . . . .
W . . . G . . . .
O R T H E E . . .
. . . . E . . . .
```

THE DINGY DINGHY

Evie doesn't last long with Scrabble
we go down to the lake with our floats

she throws her raft over the water
jumps in

I drag the yellow scuffed up dinghy
to the edge of the dock
wait for the water to calm down
scan the cracks between the boards
for mist
fog
smoke
ghost vapor

balance on the ladder
holding the dinghy steady with my toe
ease into the bottom

dip pull
  dip pull

stay clear of the broken dock

behind the abandoned house next door

> *bungee cords?*
> *I'll check the basement*
> *garage*
> *stores in town*
> *ask Mr. Glaze*
>
> *dip pull*
> *dip pull*
>
> *what a weird request*
> *Is she going to tie*
> *the rowboat back together?*

"Jayce,"
Evie calls
sounding like she's yelling down a hole:
"Jayce."

my oars pop into the air
like they sprouted wings

the edges where the lake meets the shore
are very far away
I rowed myself to the middle of Lake Lucy.

A Cool and Refreshing Drink

If my heart was attached to a propeller
I'd be back at the dock in no time

Mom flaps her magazine at me from the deck
Dad and Mr. Glaze dash down the stairs

a speedboat whirrs around the bend
like a blender gone crazy

I'm going to be Lake Lucy's
Smoothie of the Week.

THE HAND OF
LAKE LUCY

I paddle the dinghy in a circle
clockwise
dig my oars into choppy waves

pulling
tugging

an invisible hand holds me in place
heat bakes my head

I dip my hand into the water
rub my sizzling face

the rocking lake
the cloudless sky
houses peeking from trees
docks jutting into the water
blur together

a giant smeary
jigsaw puzzle.

THE BREATH OF
LAKE LUCY

The motorboat blender
grinds louder

slap pull
  slap pull

row myself in a circle
counterclockwise
squeeze hard to
wring my eyes clear

a breeze blasts my neck
the hot breath of an angry wind

pushes me to the middle of the lake
into the path of the speedboat.

IF I EVER GET BACK TO SHORE

The speedboat slows
bouncing on whitecaps
propelling waves the size of
pitchers' mounds at me

a zombie guy
staring over the bow
revs the boat

wave to him

happy I'm
outside the lake
can't escape
the speedboat's wake

swallow a mouthful of water
as I hug the dinghy

finding six bungee cords
is going to be a piece of cake
compared to this adventure.

Lake Lucy Lullaby

I cough
cup my hands
bale out water
from my dinghy

Lake Lucy is quiet
except for the screams of my parents

point the back of my raft toward them
row-two-three
row-two-three

sing a shaky lullaby
to Lake Lucy
under my breath
to the rhythm of the oars:

    Go to sleeeeep
    go to sleeeeep
    shut your big
    waaatery eyes!

my arms feel like they're stuffed with sand

the dinghy bumps into the dock

Mr. Glaze beams at me like I won a race:
"Good job, Jayce. That boater's possessed."

Dad reaches down to steady the raft

"Really? He's really possessed?"
glance at Evie cowering behind Mom

"Like my putter today. Couldn't sink
a putt worth beans."
he pokes Evie in the shoulder

"Who's that guy in the speedboat, Tom?"
Dad grabs my hand
yanks me up and out of the dinghy

Mom hugs me

"He's from town. Owns Doogie's
Dollar Emporium across the lake."
Mr. Glaze aims his arm over the water
"Always been a jerk. A mostly harmless jerk."

Mostly? "That's Doogie?"
I ask

"Doogie is his sister. His name
is Bartholomew. Mew for short."

I snort:
"He must like cats."

Dad pulls the dinged-up dinghy
from the lake:
"Be more careful, Jayce. You shouldn't

be in the middle of the lake in the dinghy.
It's dangerous out there. These little
rafts and such aren't meant to cross the lake."

Evie stands next to me
dripping over my feet
shivering
takes my hand

"Okay."
give two quick squeezes to Evie's hand:
"I'm getting changed."

"Me, too."
Evie's flip-flops slap their way upstairs
when we get to the kitchen
she hiccups:
"The ghost has Mr. Crunch, doesn't he?"

I Score a
Bungee Cord

I stare at my enormous toes
spread on the kitchen floor
like rejected ping pong paddles

"I knew the ghost had Mr. Crunch."
she pounds the table:
"What are you going to do?
Tell Mom and Dad."

"Wait a minute. Let me try first.
I think I can get Mr. Crunch back."

Evie stomps into the hallway by our rooms:
"What did the note say?"

"He wants six two-foot-long bungee cords."
or more precisely
the note read:

> 'leave 6 2-foot bungee cords in the mailbox or the lizard
> is toast'.

Evie selects a towel from the closet:
"Bungee cords? Like what Dad uses
to strap the luggage to the roof of the car?"

clap my hands:
"Yes! You're brilliant."
dash out the door to the garage
leaving Evie with a dark empty mailbox mouth.

*Does one four-foot bungee cord
equal two two-foot bungee cords?*

ONE OR TWO DOWN,
FIVE OR SIX TO GO

Evie comes in my room
as I stash the bungee cord
under my bed
that I found in the car:
"If the ghost has Mr. Crunch, he's next door."

"When can you get him? Can you go now?"

"Not now. Everyone's watching me."

study her:
"Why are you so hung up
on that crazy looking lizard?"

Evie picks on a loose thread
on my bedspread:
"He knows my secrets."

wait

"He's so cute."

harumph

you mean Noah's so cute

the screen door snaps shut

"Jayce? Where are you?"
Mom calls

whisper to Evie:
"I promise I'll go next door soon."

lean on the windowsill in my room
stare at the house next door
not even the sunlight touches it

shiver
must be from my wet bathing suit.

LATER THAT AFTERNOON

Mom drops us at Doogie's Dollar Emporium
with our pockets full of allowance money
while she goes to the grocery store

Evie wanders around the school supply section
picking out colored pencils
and pens that smell like fruit

I glance at the cashier to see if it's
the zombie who almost
blenderized me in the lake
but it's a lady with pink and blue hair

blue hair
doesn't count as a blue head

go straight to the hardware aisle
grab whatever they have
two twenty-four-inch bungee cords
two thirty-six-inch bungee cords

if I time that whole thing right
I can stuff the mailbox

with a delivery later today
get Mr. Crunch back by noon tomorrow

I throw in a missile launcher
candy for future bribes
and a pack of Pokémon cards

while we wait on a bench for Mom
I text Blas about the letter
and what happened to
Evie's favorite stuffed animal

feel brave
if only for a second
thinking I can go in the house myself
and rescue Mr. Crunch

the brave feeling melts away
getting to the mailbox is hard enough

I just want to
figure out the phantom
decode my dreams
unlock Lake Lucy's legacy

that's not too much to ask

oh and yeah
get back Mr. Crunch.

Dear Ghost,

I found bungee cords. That's a very strange request. Leave the lizard in the mailbox. That's our agreement.

Signed,

J

A Humidifier in the Mailbox

While everybody's getting dinner ready
I sneak out the front door
Dad is right
the grass by the driveway is trampled big time
take another route to the mailbox

inhale a giant breath
sucking in the energy
and courage that leaked out of Evie

feet drag as I set out for the road
the letter and bag of bungee cords weigh a ton
the driveway is a giant treadmill
I'm moving
but not getting anywhere

after a hundred years
I stop in front of the mailbox
trees rustle like an empty bag of potato chips

no ghostie's hand grabs me
as I stuff everything into the shadowy hole

but cool vapor
like the humidifier we use
when we have colds
curls from the opening

I spring backwards into the street
a car zooms by honking at me

fly to the house
like I'm running to home plate

crumple in a chair
wait for my heart to stop thudding
before I go out to the deck to eat
grilled cheese and pickles
too bad I'm not hungry.

ROCKET MAN

After I don't eat much
take my rocket launcher
to the front yard
as an excuse to watch
the haunted mailbox

hoping
Lucy checked her mail
and Mr. Crunch is hanging
out the opening

the red flag droops
no mist drifts from it
the tree in the front yard
eats all my rockets

go to my room
reread the letters
scribble in my notebook
afraid I missed something in her answers
afraid I can't get her what she wants
afraid I'll spend the rest of my life
afraid.

WHO IS OPAL?

I'm swinging in the hammock
under the deck
falling rain sounds like
hundreds of tiny drummers

Lake Lucy overflows
water swallows the dock
creeps closer to the steps
when I run into our house somehow
I wind up in the house next door

Lucy drifts in the boat
in her dreary
dusky
dusty
living room
petting Mr. Crunch
with her pointy red fingernails

frantic white bats flap toward me
a circling whirlwind of letters

I rip an envelope open

my face is drenched
the writing is blurry

I stare at the paper
before my dream melts away:

Opal! She was my precious girl! She loved me best! Not the wicked one you seek. I won't rest and neither will you, until you get me Opal's rowboat that was named for her and her dear collar that she once wore. No one can help me but you. They refuse to listen, like they did all those years ago, when I wanted one of her pups. They're stubborn and cruel, but you hear me. My own brother won't listen. No one listens! Those aren't just things. They're mine because Opal should have been mine! How I miss her. Return her boat and collar to me at the bottom of the lake.

"What things? Who's Opal?"

when I awake
my hands wrench pages in my notebook
like I'm trying to read my dream.

MIDNIGHT MADNESS

I slide to the edge of my bed
smooth the pages
write in my beat-up notebook
what I remember about Lucy's letter
which isn't much:
Opal! get her things to me

One ghost
Petrifies me
And her name is
Lucy

I creep to the window
a sliver of light splits my curtains
like a laser beam

the moon glows high above the treetops
as if somebody on the other side of the sky
ripped a crooked hole in a black curtain
light pours out
on the scraggly bushes next door

two bright spots whip from one window
to the other
stop and stare at me
double laser beam eyes
of a wild animal
watching
then slipping away.

A TRIP OUTSIDE THAT STINKS

The next morning
I drag myself out of bed
with the awful thought
of going to the mailbox

Evie's eyes look like she stared
through my binoculars all night
hollow and blood shot

she slaps her spoon
up and down in her cereal
sending speckles of milk over the table

"Want to play catch?"
I ask wiping milk from my shirt

"Catch?"
Evie looks through me
as if I'm the one made of mist:
"No."

I fiddle with my napkin:
"I'll be right back."

Mom whirls around from the sink:
"Where do you think you're going?"

"Outside to see how hot it is."

"You can do that out back,"
she hands me a plastic bag:
"Put this in the trash can
on the side of the house. Thank you."

the bag is plenty stinky
drop it in the metal trash can
toss the lid back on

walk down the driveway
and onto the street to face the mailbox

the red flag is half up
pointing at me.

My Inside-Head Voice
Gives Advice... Again

I let the house's mysterious draw on my legs
propel me towards the mailbox

bend down to peer in
nothing shoved in the back
no blue lizard toes
no letter from me
no bag of bungee cords
not even mist

cram my hand in the back
until I feel the crisp edge of a piece of paper:

> *meet me at 8pm on the back porch.*
> *don't tell anybody & don't be late.*

shove the note in my pocket
hustle to our driveway

a voice from the back of my brain
that I don't recognize

but sounds a little like Evie again
says:
(Take a tour of the place now
and get it over with).

My Inside-Head Voice
Won't Shut Up

My left foot starts
for the house next door
(Come on, Jayce. You can do this.)

Evie's face
and empty eyes
wiggle in front of me
like a mirage

my other foot joins the first one
on the grass
but I pivot and flee along
the side of the house
to the underside of the deck
(Hey! Wrong way!)

on the swing
I read the note again:

meet me next door.

he's not there now
I wouldn't say to Blas,

'Meet me at my house'
if I'm home, right?
I'd say, 'Come on over.'

that means it's an empty house
(Nothing scary about that!)
I'd rather be eating a ham sandwich

I text Blas to see what he thinks
he agrees with the inside-head voice
with many thumbs-up emojis

I spring from the swing
before I know what my feet are doing
they carry me through the bushes
to the porch next door

a blue tarp sags between two sawhorses
the door to the porch
with its screen hanging like a loose sail
is all that's between me and Lucy's hide-out.

WELCOME TO MY DREAM HOUSE

The screen door pushes open easily
I stand in the screened-in porch
crispy leaves from years of autumns
pile in the corners
the stone floor is etched with mud

turn the knob to the back door
lean against it
locked

search under the crumbling
door mat for a key—
nothing

a cracked clay pot
with the skeleton of a dead plant
sits next to the door
I reach into the middle of it
pull out a key.

A Key Plant

The key fits in the lock
clicks after a few wiggles
I drop it back in the pot

door's stuck
doesn't budge
I shove my way inside
a loud creak from the door hinges
announces me

the musty room
is decorated with shadows
dust collects everywhere
but the weirdest thing
is the bow of a rowboat
smack in the middle
of the living room.

WITH MY OWN EYEBALLS

My eyes adjust to the dim light
filtering through dirty windows

> half rowboat/half raft
> assorted boards
> bungee cords
> giant plastic water bottles
> hammer and large nails

zoom around the house

> *I know where I am*
> *because I live it in my dreams*

opening drawers and doors
searching for anything blue

> *Mr. Crunch, where are you?*
> *Why didn't we put a tracking chip*
> *under your fur like Grandma's pit bull?*
> *Does Mom miss me? How long does*
> *it take to throw garbage away?*

when I round the corner to check upstairs
I yank off the ball at the end of the banister
stick it back on its peg
blast up the steps

a busted-up bench in one of the bedrooms
drawers that refuse to open
closets with dangling hangers

I rush down the steps and sneeze
the house shudders as it magnifies the noise
pause at the back door
hand on knob
listen to the sound of my own blood
whooshing in my head
or something else rushing through the house

my heart bangs in my chest
my throat closes

stinky garbage smell suffocates me
I look at the floor where

my feet disappear in the cool vapor
streaming under the coat closet door
swirling around my ankles
like lake water at the beach.

EVIE WANTS TO HELP

I bolt outside
slamming the door behind me

drop to the weeds
when I hear voices from my house
Mom and Dad sit on the far side of the deck

I fly across the grass
dive through the bushes

after I shake off the dirt
I climb into a swing

"Where were you?"
Evie asks from the other hammock:
"I told Mom you were getting
fishing poles in the basement."

"Next door,"
I say between gasps for air:
"I went inside."

her eyebrows shoot up

like she's trying to open her eyes better:
"You went inside? Is that why you look
like you've seen a ghost?"

I laugh like a weak hyena

"You didn't really, did you?"

"It was creepy in there.
All dusty, like a haunted house
at Halloween."
rustle the paper in my pocket:
"Read this."

Evie reads it as if she's
a boa constrictor digesting a pig:
"What do you have to help him
with that he can't do himself?"

I shrug:
"Who knows? 'He's a ghost,
not a magician.'"
I quote Blas:
"Except, I think the ghost is Lucy."

"Lucy? I believe you."

dig my toe into the dirt
push myself in the swing

Evie runs her gaze over the note again

my swing twirls
my body keeps up
with my spinning head

she bites her bottom lip:

"The house, did you see anything?"

my swing slows
we might not have twin radar
but I feel her ache for Mr. Crunch:
"It's super dark in there. I saw the rowboat.
Parts of it. The ghost's making a raft."

"Did you see anything else?"
she whispers

"Sorry."

she scrapes her feet up the steps

"I'll get him back."

Evie peeks at me from between the slats:
"I know you will. I'll help."

BLAS RETURNS TO NEW YORK

I text Blas to update him
he tells me his family is
leaving Lake Lucy today
his little brother has a fever

feel a little blue—
headed

because when
I talk or text Blas
bravery fills me
he doesn't make fun of me

he makes me feel like
I have the courage
to do scary things

I hope I do the same for him
we promise to keep-in-text

a short-term friend
can be a long-lasting friend.

Meanwhile While Mom and Dad Watch TV

At seven-forty-five that night
I get ready to meet the ghost next door

I've been nervous about seeing
the dentist every year
or the doctor when I broke my wrist
or even having baseball try-outs
but nothing like this

I call Evie on her cell phone
she mutes herself
while we stay connected
so she can hear everything going on

tuck my phone into a pocket
in my cargo shorts

Evie stations herself
by my bedroom window

I sneak down the basement stairs
the swings sway in the lake breeze
that same fishy smell fills the air

peer through the bushes

my feet won't budge
like they grew roots in the dirt
maybe the vibrations from my pounding heart
will unearth them

wipe my sweaty palms on my shorts
memories with sharp cleats
of Grandma's dark airless attic
play simultaneous games
of baseball in my stomach

uproot my feet
trudge through the bushes
try not to sound like an elephant

nod to Evie's mask-like face in my window
think of Blas's excitement
but my courage squishes out of me
like stale air from an old balloon

reach the house next door
open the screen door to the porch
consider the key from the pot
but then she'll know I was here before

knock on the door to the house
I'm about to meet the ghost of my dreams.

ON THE OTHER SIDE OF THE DOOR...

Shuffle

shuffle

Scrape
doorknob clicks

door cracks

I muscle it open
the rest of the way

step inside and sneeze.

I MEET THE GHOST

My eyes adjust to the gloom
Will she look like a drowned human?
Will she be wrapped in mist?

a saw and other tools lay near
the bow of the rowboat
on the far end of the room

a raft balances in its place
on top of giant empty water bottles

snickering

hate snickering

I whirl around

Austin the year-round boy
steps from the coat closet

"It's been you all this time?"
try to stand straight
add a few millimeters to my height:

"Give me back Evie's stuffed animal."

he strolls to the middle of the room:
"You'll get the lizard. You're going
to help me get my raft out to the lake."

I walk around the raft
balanced on the sideways water bottles:
"What's it doing in here, anyway?"

"It's a good place to work. Nobody's
lived here for ages. Used to be some
lady's house. A loner."

"Lucy. Like you."
I think out loud

Austin squeezes his fists:
"We're nothing alike. I've got
a best friend, man."

PIECE BY PIECE

Austin smooths the top of the raft
like he's petting a big dog
or new Ferrari:
"I dragged in pieces of the rowboat
stored under that tarp outside."
he points to the ceiling:
"Broke up furniture. I worked
on her all through the spring."

"Wow. Cool. All by yourself?"
I sneeze

Austin's face brightens:
"Yeah."

"What are the bungee cords for?"

he kneels
taps on the water bottles under the raft:
"To attach these empty bottles
I got from my dad's office from the
water cooler to the raft. I had a few
bungee cords of my own, but not enough."

"Amazing."
I lean over the raft:
"Why don't you get your dad
to help carry it out of here?"

he frowns:
"Bad back. And he doesn't exactly
want me to go on the water.
I want my own raft
to go around the lake. Those
dinghies are worthless."

I go to the far end of the raft:
"Okay. Let's go."

"It's not the right time."
he scowls at me

I back away:
"When is the right time?"

ANOTHER MEETING
IS SET

Austin picks a folded paper
out of his back pocket and checks it:
"Day after tomorrow.
Meet me at eight o'clock again.
Don't be late."
he jams it back

when we go to the door
the wad of paper falls out

I follow him
kick it into the coat closet

he yanks open the back door:
"We won't have much time.
Don't tell anyone
what you're doing or
that you saw me
if you still want your sister's
stuffed animal back."

"How'd you get him?"
I ask imagining him

sliding open a window
tiptoeing into Evie's room
stuffing Mr. Crunch
into a bag

he laughs:
"It fell out of all your junk
when you left the beach."

like that chunk of paper
I rub my chin:
"How'd you get the mist
in the mailbox and up
the cracks on my deck?"

his eyes widen:
"I don't know what
you're talking about."
then narrow
he smirks:
"That's my little secret."

I trip over the flowerpot
when he slams the back door
catch myself on the floor
whisper to my knee:
"Evie, I'm coming back."

THE GHOST WRITER'S
GHOST WRITER

I concentrate on wrenching my legs
away from the house
and break the invisible chains
the house uses to tether me
to its creepy self

my legs fly over the grass
under the deck
up the stairs to the bedroom
the TV blares from the living room
Evie sits on my bed
hugging her knees

"Did you hear all that?
The ghost writer has a ghost writer—Austin."

Evie almost looks normal:
"I never thought it was a real ghost.
Why do you suppose he wants you
to help him night after tomorrow
instead of tonight?"

"I don't know. But I'm going over

early again tomorrow. He took a fat wad of paper
out of his pocket and looked at it. When he went
to put it back, it fell out."

"What do you think it was?"

I shrug:
"Maybe it's a clue to where he's hiding Mr. Crunch.
Or what he's really up to. Why would he go
to all the trouble of building a raft
if his dad might see it on the lake? I'll sneak over tomorrow
to have a look."

Evie's eyes light up like twin flashlights

feel hopeful
go to bed on time
lay awake
scared feeling wiggles into my head
circles round and round
like a cat trying to get comfortable
in a spot of sun
the cat is Austin

not convinced he told the truth
about the mist-through-the-dock-boards trick

he's real close to acting like
that fractured flowerpot
a jagged split giving way
all the dried-up dirt and roots spilling out
maybe a few dead horse flies too

Austin acts like—
his pitch overshot
his mind's in a knot
a cracked flowerpot.

Evie's Perfect Timing

The next morning
Evie skips past my room:
"Cinnamon rolls for breakfast!"

I turn in my bed
face the wall
looks like things are back to normal
I didn't even have a nightmare

glance at the clock next to my bed
I'll go back to Lucy's house
after breakfast to check out
that wad of paper Austin dropped

the sweet smell of cinnamon
pulls me into the kitchen
like a fish on a hook

"We have a big day planned, sport."
Dad pours himself a coffee

icing drips from my fingers
I know. Eat breakfast,

break into the house next door...

"We're going to the other side
of the lake and spend the day
with the Hydes."

I choke

"Easy, fella."
Dad pats me on the back:
"Pack your swimsuit
and maybe your pajamas.
We might not get back till late."

"We're going today?"
my fingers hover over my plate

"We'll leave in a half hour."
Dad hands me napkins

"Can't we go tomorrow?"
scrape the icing off my hand

right on cue
Evie makes it to the bathroom
to barf.

A BUCKET OF WORMS

After Mom reschedules
with the Hydes
the morning and afternoon drag
like a fishing pole baited with
a bucket of worms
without the worms

Mom and Dad hover around us
I can't get to Lucy's house

"Buddy, do you want to go for a paddle?"
Dad peers over his little reading glasses:
"I inflated the dinghy if you promise to stay close."

I press my nose against the screen door:
"I don't feel like it."

"How about going to the dollar store again?"
Mom asks:
"I'm going to pick up stamps at the post office
and Pepto-Bismol."

and risk another chance to meet

the zombie speedboat captain?
no, thanks
then I'll need the stomach medicine:
"That's okay."
feel the waffle marks left
on my nose from the screen:
"Maybe I'll play a game with Evie."

"That'll be nice."
Mom sticks a ribbon in her book:
"Can I get you anything in town?"
she asks Dad

"A bucket of worms!"

"You'll have to come with me.
I'm not going to pick up any worms."
Mom wrinkles her nose:
"Don't go in the lake alone, Jayce."

"We should go now,"
Dad says:
"We only have an hour. I think they close at six."

Mom slides the screen door aside
steps into the kitchen:
"You and Evie will be all right, won't you?
We won't be long."

"We'll be fine."
I follow her through the kitchen

she reaches in her pocket
pulls her phone out
shakes it:
"We're just a text or call away."

"I told you we'll be fine."

she stuffs the phone in her purse:
"Evie needs something
to settle her stomach.
She needs to rest. She's realizing that
the world isn't perfect and
things don't always go our way.
Someone probably stole Mr. Crunch."

"Mom, I said okay."

she picks up the car keys from the desk:
"Tell her we'll be home within the hour.
Keep the doors locked and don't
answer the house phone."

"I don't think the house phone is hooked up,"
I say

she slings her purse on her shoulder:
"Right. Call us if there's a problem."
pats my cheek

"All set?"
asks Dad

when the car leaves
I burst into Evie's room:
"I'm going to the ex-haunted house again."

SHIVER ME TIMBERS!

When the car leaves
I burst into Evie's room
hand Evie her cell phone
from her nightstand:
"I'll call you when I get inside."

hustle downstairs
wait under our deck
close my right eye pirate-style
long enough for my pupil to shrink

dash to the nearly screened-in porch
dig my hand into the pot
the dead plant scratches my fingers

the key is gone
Austin must've kept it
when he left yesterday

let Evie know I'm on the porch
brace my shoulder against the door

Unless Austin's already inside?

Hold up.

listen for shuffling
tapping
breathing

     that's mine
     I'm too scared
     to be scared
     of the dark

shove harder
the flimsy lock gives up
and I fall inside.

Ahoy!

I brush my knees
open my pirate eye that's already
used to darkness
murmur to Evie:
"I'm inside!"

hunt in the coat closet
until I find the wad of paper
a folded bus schedule
from the Stanley bus depot

tell Evie that Austin's planning a trip
he circled the twice weekly departure time
five-oh-six PM to its final stop
in Sacramento, California
a long way from Lake Lucy, Virginia

whisper to Evie:
"Can you hear me? Why did
he make a raft to take a bus?"

Evie's voice shakes:
"I hear you. I don't know. Have

you seen Mr. Crunch?"

"Not yet."
I tuck the schedule in my left knee pocket:
"We pass a bus station in town."

she sighs:
"He can't drive, so he's rafting
across the lake..."

"... to take a bus. Alone."

"Why alone? How do you know
he'll be alone?"

I edge closer to the center
of the room:
"Have you ever seen him
with a friend?"
examine the remains of the rowboat
use my cell phone as a flashlight
Opal is painted on the bow in faded pink

the ghost mentioned Opal in my dream-letter
but that ghost isn't real
unless...

if I was a cat
my fur would be standing up straight

Evie's short breaths
pull me back:
"Maybe he has a phantom friend.
Like online?"

"And Austin's going to meet him.
We've got to stop him."

AUSTIN IS READY TO PULL ANCHOR

I reach for the flap on my knee pocket
stiffen as Austin appears in the room

"That's you making all the noise.
I thought a raccoon broke in again."
he threw something bulky on the sofa:
"What are you doing here?"

chills straighten my spine
hope Evie didn't forget to mute herself
and doesn't give me talking pants:
"My parents are gone. I thought
this was as good a time as any
to help you move the raft."

Austin studies his cell phone
tucks it in a zippered pocket:
"Why not? This might work out better
but we have to hurry."
he moves past me to the door:
"How'd you get in here?"

"The door gave way."

I back toward the raft

"This house is about to fall apart."
he opens the door wide:
"Were you talking to someone?"

"Ghosts?"
I laugh:
"Just myself. Bad habit."
Quit babbling.

when Austin stands with his hands on his hips
he looks nine feet tall:
"You didn't bring anybody, did you?"

"Only me. That's who I talk to. Me."

he stares at me with his silvery gray eyes:
"Creepy. And they say I have problems."

"Do they?"
my eyes widen
hope Evie heard that:
"Do you have an oar for this thing?"

"Right here."
he picks it up from the sofa
sets it under a bungee cord strapped to the raft

"What's in there?"
point to the backpack

he squints at me:
"You ask too many questions.
Pick her up, and we'll try to squeeze
through the door. Try not to scrape her."

"Wait a minute. What about Mr. Crunch?"
I grip the end
test the weight of the raft

"Who?"
he squints at me

"The blue lizard. When do I get it back?"

Austin adjusts the leather band on his wrist:
"When we get the raft to the water,
I'll tell you where he is. You really
like your sister to go to all this trouble for her."

"I guess. We're twins."

he wipes his hands on his shorts:
"You're lucky. You have somebody
to talk to and stuff."

"I don't understand her half the time."

he squats by his end of the raft:
"Man, you don't get it. In a couple years,
she'll be bringing home her friends."

She brings them home all the time. So?
I crouch to pick up my end of the raft
something heavy crashes on the second floor
pounds down each step like a giant dead head
wearing a football helmet of steel.

Not a Peg Leg but a Peg Head

I stop breathing
Austin and I stare at each other
over the length of the raft

whatever dropped down the steps
rolls around the foyer
bouncing off the walls
A head? A blue head?

"See what that is,"
he picks up the hammer

"Me?"
I squeak

Austin peers around my shoulder:
"Go."

when I get to the stairs
I breathe again:
"It's only this wooden ball thing
that sits on the railing."
I show the softball-sized ball to Austin

who followed me to the staircase:
"It came loose from the handrail at the top
and banged down the stairs."

"There's never been a wooden ball up there."
Austin says

my eyes follow the curve of the banister
as it disappears into the wall

Austin points to the peg on the handrail
on the bottom of the steps:
"It goes here."

"How did it get upstairs?"
my mouth dries up

Austin wiggles it on the peg:
"Beats me. Let's get the raft out of here.
Or your sister will never see
her blue lizard again."

Ship in a Bottle

The only thing I hear are
our own grunts
as we hoist the clumsy raft

with four giant water bottles
strapped to the underside
and waddle across the floor
bang up the door frame

"I don't think this is working."
like getting a ship out of a bottle
my face prickles from sweat
as I put down my end of the raft

"Hey, dude."
Austin sets his end down

"Jayce,"
I say

"Jayce, we're getting this raft on the water."
his expression mirrors Dad's
when he sees my room a few days

after I've cleaned it
and it looks like it exploded. Again:
"Go through the door at an angle."

pick up my end
afraid my arms
will rip out of their sockets
sneeze:
"What's that smell?"

"You're making things up."
Austin wrinkles his nose:
"Man, that does stinks.
Like moldy, rotten fish."

my eyes water:
"Where's it coming from?
Maybe your raccoon died."

"Let's hurry."
Austin buries his nose in his shoulder

"Do you have a remote-control
fog maker?"

Austin pants as he steps
near the door
with his end of the raft:
"Huh?"

"I know, dry ice. We used it in
a school play. It makes this cool
fog that creeps along the ground.
Where'd you get it?"

Austin sets his end on the doorstep:
"What are you talking about now?"

I put my end down
point to the closet:
my air-conditioned feet wiggle
as mist pours from the door
like steam from a witch's cauldron.

Heave Ho!

Austin's fierce expression fades
as he yanks up his end
of the raft:
"Let's go!"

I don't know why I worry
about Evie not hearing us

Austin's voice is plenty loud.
I should worry about Mom and Dad
hearing us from across the lake.

THE LAUNCH

When we tilt the raft
on the diagonal
it sails right through
the back door

Austin rips through a screened wall
in the porch
and we're outside
the rest of the trip is downhill

  for real

the slope to the lake
covered in weeds
snag our sneakers
until we set the raft in the water

Austin rushes to the house
while I hold the end of the raft
with my foot
to keep it from floating away

  I'm sure my numb arms

have stretched two inches

he removes the oar
from the bungee cord
replaces it with his backpack

"I think it might rain. Rafting's
no fun if you're soaked."
a last-ditch effort
to keep him from crossing
to the bus depot

while Austin steadies himself
on the raft
I ask:
"Why'd you answer my letters?"

"Something to do."
holding onto the broken dock
he takes a wide stance in the middle
of his creation:
"It gets boring here. I'm the only
year-round kid on the lake. Especially
in winter. But I made a new friend
I'm going to see."

the hairs on my neck poke up

"So long, Jayce."
Austin pushes the dock with the oar:
"I'll send you a postcard."

"Really? From where?"
I ask

he shakes his head

he wrenches the oar through the water
reaches the end of the broken-down dock

I pick my way over the broken boards:
"Hey, who's Opal?"

he sways and adjusts his feet:
"A dog."

Dog? I guess Lucy named her boat
after her dog.
"Austin, where's the lizard?"

"Upstairs in a drawer."
he calls over his shoulder
wobbling on the raft:
"Good luck in that house."
and laughs.

TICK TICK TICK

Mist tumbles from the house
covers my ankles
musty and sour
like the far-left outfield
that's been wet too long
and turned algae-green

I trip in the mist covered living room
fumble for my cell phone in my pocket:
"Evie, are you there?"
when I round the bend to the steps
the ball falls off the banister again
drops like a bowling ball on the floor

"Evie?"
check my phone's battery
five percent
not a good time to run out of power

"Evie. Do you hear me?"
dart into the first bedroom
drag open all the drawers

Evie answers:
"Jayce, what's going on?
I saw you and that kid
dragging a raft down to the lake."

"Mr. Glaze's son is running away
from home. Today."
recheck the bus schedule:
"The next bus to California
leaves at five o'clock."

Evie gasps:
"Oh, no! It's after four-thirty."

Flying Lizard

No Mr. Crunch in any of the drawers
sneeze my way down the hall
to the other bedroom

Dad calls on my cell phone
missed two calls from him already

so many stuck drawers
I beat on the lowest with my fists
brace my feet against the legs
yank on the handles

back muscles scream
drawer flies out
hits me on the chin

Mr. Crunch pops in the air
like a fly ball
wearing my Diamondbacks
baseball cap I lost when
Austin tripped me at the beach

scoop him up

squash the hat on my head:
"Am I glad to see you."

"Jayce, Jayce,"
Evie squawks:
"Dad wants to talk to you."

"Tell him I'm in the bathroom,
and meet me on our dock
with binoculars."

tuck Mr. Crunch under my arm
bolt down the steps
into the sticky fingers
of putrid freezing vapor
in the living room
as my cell phone battery dies.

SUFFOCATING GLOOM
VERSUS SUFFOCATING
DOOM

A thick cloud covers
the living room floor
to my waist
pours like a cottony river
out of the closet door
onto the porch

    being stuck in an airless
    dark
    closed attic
    almost sounds like
    a good time
    next to this

trip on a chair leg
submerge in the cold whiteness
pull my T-shirt over my mouth
grope for a clear space
to scramble out the door

foggy swirl drains into the back yard
with Mr. Crunch safe under my arm

I dash to our dock
the fog seeps along the surface
of the lake heading for Austin.

STILL AFLOAT

An ear-splitting squeal
gushes from Evie
when she sees Mr. Crunch
Austin probably hears her

I grab her cell phone
hold it to my chest:
"My phone's dead."

Evie points to my face
while clutching Mr. Crunch:
"You're bleeding."

"Do you have my spy glasses?"
whisper to Evie
take a deep breath:
"Dad, can I call you back?"

"What's going on there?
You better not have been in the lake.
Or, snooping around next door,"
Dad says

take the binoculars from Evie
swing the cord over my head:
"Of course, not."
dash to the rocky path
along the shore
to get a better view of the open water

shade my eyes
find the raft
Austin hasn't sunk
he's a dot with a foggy tail
like a vapor trail from an airplane
only his boat isn't making the exhaust

the mist pursues him
Lucy the ghost is after Austin.

PHONE LIKE A FISH

I hold the cell phone in one hand
binoculars in the other
either Austin is resting
or in shock
because he's not paddling:
"We're just goofing around, Dad."

Dad: *yak yak yak*

something furry brushes my elbow
Mr. Crunch stares at me with
his felt tongue sticking out
of his grinning mouth

Dad: *blah blah blah*

Evie hands me a tissue for my face
she wet in the lake:
"What's that white stuff behind Austin?"

I whisper back:
"It's the ghost next door.
She's after Austin."

not him
she's after something else
what thing?
two things?
red thing
blue thing
I can't read the ghost letter
because it's in my dream

the binoculars dangle from my neck

"Everything's fine,"
I say to Dad
dabbing my chin

Dad: *jabber jabber jabber*

Evie gawks at me
whisper-shouts:
"Austin's running away
and a ghost is chasing him."
she points to the cell phone:
"Tell Dad."

shake my head
the phone slips out of my hands
like a fish
lands on a rock
splits in half
each piece bounces
disappears into the scrubby shrubs.

IF MR. CRUNCH COULD SPEAK

Evie shrieks:
"Now we can't call Dad,
and Austin will get away.
Or be caught by the ghost."

    peering through the binoculars
    tiny Austin rocks on the raft
    caught in the middle of my nightmare

Evie digs through the bushes
scratching her arms:
"I'll look for the phone. Look for the battery."

    mist trails from the house
    across the weeds
    rolling on the water
    heading toward Austin:
    "Lucy, what do you want?"

Evie's face blanks
her eyes roll upward in her head
mist curls from her mouth
thick and coiled

she speaks like a horse fly
or Mr. Crunch if he could speak:
"Happy kids don't run away.
No matter how old they are."

wave my hands in her face:
"What's happening to you?"

"Protect him and protect yourself,"
the voice rasps

shake her arm:
"Evie, what are you saying?"

"Save the boy. He's not like his mother."

"What's wrong with Austin's mother?"

Evie coughs:
"Don't stand there, Jayce. Do something."
she dives into the bushes.

Hold On, Austin!

The lake glints
in the late afternoon sun

Austin braces his feet
on the floor of the raft

a familiar whirring buzzes
beyond the alcove

Austin is running away from home
and running toward a 'friend'
I know the ghost needs my help

    thanks to her possessing Evie

the ghost needs me to help Austin

    not all ghosts are (completely) scary
    not all 'friends' are buddies.

A Fight with a Bush

My arm is the right length
to reach the slippery cell phone

between two large rocks
in front of a spiky bush

graze it with my fingertips
press further into the bush

its branches push me away
I grab the phone

after the bush slaps me
in the face

Evic wipes the phone clean on her shirt:
"Find the battery!"

Meanwhile...

...Austin bobs on his raft
not paddling
alone
except for the buzz
of horse flies
and one very large speedboat.

CELL PHONE RESTART

I scan the shrubs
pounce on the battery

Evie gives it
a good rubbing

snaps it all together
pushes the 'on' button

nothing—
two dead cell phones.

THE CHASE

I whip the spy glasses
off my neck
hand them to Evie:
"Keep trying to get
the phone to work."
dart to the dock
kick my sandals off
throw the dingy dinged-up
dinghy into the water

"What are you doing?"
Evie yells

flop into the dinghy:
"Going after Austin."

my shorts soak up water
from its bottom
tug on the oars
head for the mist wondering
if this is a crazy dream

before I couldn't peek in

the window of the house next door

now I'm chasing the vapor trail
of a ghost

and a run-away kid who's
more like a row-away kid

wind shoves the dinghy
chills me
choppy waves splatter
my back

the closer I get to the mist
the more my oars grind
into the hard surface of the water
the calmer the waves become

because water doesn't move
when it freezes.

RUNAWAY SCHOOL BUS

When I check on Austin
his raft is drift-sliding
but not fast enough

the vapor rolls
and drags itself
across the water
like a giant white slug

"I'm coming to get you,"
I shout over my shoulder
hope he doesn't think
it's the mist threatening him

hope Lucy doesn't think
I'm threatening her

Austin wakes up
paddles like he's
being chased
which he is
by two of us
I row double time

slam crunch
slam crunch

I crack through the thin ice
line up alongside the vapor

the whirring noise surges
the air vibrates
cracks shoot through thin ice
forming over the lake

heat is sucked out of my body
I shiver

then spot what's growling
as it heads toward Austin
as big and fast as
a bus late for school.

RUNAWAY SPEEDBOAT

A big speedboat skims the water
on the far side of the arm of mist
Austin and the boat are headed for a collision

fright helps me paddle faster:
"Austin, jump!"
my oars crack the ice into mini glaciers

fog tickles the end of the raft

　　"I can't."
　　Austin howls

fog sneaks onto his raft
like a thief ready to steal it

"Jump in the lake and swim to my boat."
I shout

　　"I can't swim,"
　　he hollers

he didn't say that

a kid who spends his
entire life at a lake
must be able to swim

the mist curls on the bottom
of Austin's raft
inches toward his feet
"It wants your raft."

    he shudders

the speedboat's engine roars
the captain can't see us for the cloud

the ice is too thick to paddle closer
I throw Austin the rope I use
to tie the dinghy to the dock:
"Grab this and jump into the water."

    his arms dangle
    like a helpless marionette
    as he watches
    the rope slips off the raft
    mist climbs to his waist

I reel in the rope
throw it at him
hitting him in the chest:
"Grab it."

    he snaps awake
    winds the rope
    around his hand
    tests the ice off the raft
    stutter steps
    plummets through the surface

I tug the oars
with all my might
dragging Austin through the water

    hand-over-hand
    he climbs the rope
    coughing and sputtering
    flings one shaking arm
    over the end of the dinghy

"Kick,"
I yell:
"Keep kicking."

    he scissor-kicks

wrench the oars
through the waves

fog envelopes the raft
blue water cooler bottles
pop one by one from
their bungee cords
bounce on the water
bob away

on the other side of the mist
the roar of the speedboat
blocks out every other lake sound.

THE TOILET BOWL IN
THE LAKE

I didn't let up rowing
even when we're
a safe distance from
Austin's raft

as the white speedboat
with its blood-red band
plows through the mist
a crack explodes

"Take cover!"
I yell

Austin gasps and submerges
holding onto the rope

I drop the oars
shield my head with my arms

splintered wood surges into the sky
as the speedboat shoots through the fog

broken parts of the raft

pelt the lake like missiles
chunks smack the dinghy
bounce off

Austin rescues an oar
the air smells of gasoline and oil

"Are you okay?"
I ask

the speedboat slows and cruises
half a football field away
its engine cuts off
and the lake quiets

Austin hands me the oar
from the water:
"I'm okay."
he coughs

I drop it into the bottom of the dinghy:
"Let me help you get on board."
yank on his belt loops
he slides in like a seal

with the added weight
the dinghy sinks lower

cup my hands around my mouth:
"Help,"
I yell to the speedboat

Austin waves:
"Over here."

a voice rises from the mist:
"Opal."

"Do you hear that?"
Austin scans the lake

"Opal."
the mist gathers the wrecked
raft floating on the water
sweeps the pieces together
like Evie with her gel pens
a mother hen with her precious chicks

the lake gurgles as the mist
and raft fragments plunge under water
like an emptying toilet
round and round

the splintered shards
of wood and ice spiral
before the lake flushes them.

To Row Oar Not
to Row

Austin snatches a stray board
from the swift current
heading toward the vortex:
"Start rowing. It's dragging us down."

we paddle canoe-style
me with an oar
Austin with the board

behind us
mist creeps over the waves
the air chills

"Row harder."
Austin yells

as I dig the oar into the water
I can't tell if we're rowing
as we drift toward the drain
pretty soon
we'll be sucked
into the swirling whirlpool.

To Retreat Oar Not to Retreat

I glance over my shoulder
icy fingers of mist arch over Austin

ready to pluck him into the lake
thick strands of mist

coil around the wood in his hands
"Throw that scrap overboard," I yell

"No," Austin plunges the board
into the water like an oar

drop my oar into the bottom of the dinghy
wrestle the board from him

not before piercing my hands with splinters:
"Lucy wants every piece of the raft."

line up my shoulder with the whirlpool
pitch the board javelin-style into the watery coil

fog hangs in the air like it's
trying to decide to capsize us or leave

slowly shrinks from the sinking dinghy
heads toward the drain

slips into the hole in the lake
like the scrawny tail of a white rat.

THE SINKING FEELING
THAT IT'S NOT OVER

Seagulls screech in the distance
No, it's Evie.

I wave to her as we bob on the water
our nightmare is over
the whole lake sighs

"It doesn't matter about the board anyway,"
Austin says

"Did you find the other oar?"
I pluck splinters from my palm

"We don't need it."
Austin points to a hole in the raft:
"We're sinking."

the sighing sound comes from the tear
in our dinghy

I poke my finger in the hole:
"The bit about not being able to swim.
That's a joke, right?"

Austin shakes his head

the pointy bow of the speedboat
angles toward the sky
it's sinking
that explains why he isn't saving us

Captain Zombie shouts at the lake
as he rows toward the opposite shore

hand Austin the oar:
"I'll kick from behind,
while you paddle."

slip into the lake
hang on to the raft
I'm not a fast swimmer
never won any races
but I always finish.

The Long Way Home

It feels like swimming on a water treadmill
going nowhere and spending a lot of effort

I pull myself alongside the drowning dinghy:
"Let me have the rope."

Austin loops the free end
knots it

I slip it around my waist
swim in front of the dinghy
Evie jumps up and down on the dock
like it has springs

turn to check on Austin
but all that's left of the dinghy
is a yellow puff:
"Austin, dude. Where are you?
Austin?"

"I'm still here."
he puffs behind the dinghy
clings to the only part

that has air

the words—
NOT TO BE USED AS A LIFE PRESERVER
printed across it

"Hang on, we're almost there."
I lie
my legs tingle like they're on fire
it hurts to breathe
as if a javelin is stuck in my side

the harder I try to get to the dock
the further away it seems
roll on my back to rest
the sun stabs my eyes
so I close them

"Are you giving up?" Austin shouts

water spurts from my mouth like a fountain
I tread in place:
"No way. Start kicking."
dive under the surface toward Evie
wiggle like a fish
hoping to jumpstart the trip
back to the dock
my waist burns as the rope scrapes it

Austin climbs on top
parts of it pop out under his arms
the weight of the shrunken dinghy
drags it down

Austin sputters and spits out water
I don't have the energy
to say anything encouraging

my lungs are about to burst

I tow Austin close enough
for Evie to throw the life preserver

"Catch this," Evie calls

I wave one arm overhead as she flings it toward us
hitting Austin in the face

he should count himself lucky
that's all she does considering
he stole Mr. Crunch in the first place

the force knocks his head back
he disappears under the water.

WHEN YOUR SISTER IS A BEAR

I take a great breath
swim back to Austin
tangled in the deflated dinghy

push him up
he bobs on the surface
hangs like a limp towel
on the last bit of dinghy

curl my arm through
the doughnut hole of the
life preserver and
slap it over his head
his eyes are red and dazed
but he holds on

"Haul us in, Evie," I pant

Evie digs her heels into the dock
yanks the cord attached to the life preserver
she's as strong as a bear
two bears

when she pulls us alongside the dock
she lays down on the dock
holds Austin steady
while I help him climb the ladder

Austin and I fling ourselves on the hot boards
Evie's Magic Mirror eyes glow
as she clings to Mr. Crunch:
"Are you all right, Jayce?"
she bends over me

nod and sit up:
"Were you able to call Dad?"

she holds out her hand
angry dad noises spark
from the cell phone

I clear my throat:
"Dad, listen to me."

"What's going on there?
After we were cut off,
Evie told me some crazy tale
about Mr. Glaze's son rowing
to California," he squawks

"It's a long story. Austin rebuilt
a rowboat into a raft in
the empty house next door,
and I helped him take it down to the lake."
the wound on my chin
from the dresser drawer stings
like a horse fly bite

"You've been in the abandoned house
with Austin?"

Dad doesn't need a phone

Dad lowers his voice:
"Wait. How do you know him?
He's kind of a loner. That's why
Tom and I took him golfing."

I cover my mouth with my hand
turn away from Austin
speak into the phone:
"He was rowing to the bus depot
across the lake. He planned to go
to California on the five o'clock bus
to meet some new friend."

"In California? We've got
to stop him," Dad says

"It's okay. He didn't go. He's on
our dock with us. Call Mr. Glaze."
wrap myself in a towel

"We'll talk more when
Mom and I get home."
Dad clicks off.

ONE MORE THING

Evie wants to know
what happened on the lake

I peel off my shirt
and tell her

she chews her lips
"There really is a ghost."

I open my mouth to tell Evie
she was a messenger for the ghost

    maybe I'll tell her later

she steals a glance at
the deserted house
clear of mist
looking as miserable as Austin

he sits with a beach towel
hanging on his head:
"I never believed in ghosts
until now. That explains

a lot of weird things
that happened in the house."

I perk up
want to ask Austin about
flying lanterns but don't think
this is a good time:
"We have one more thing to do.
Help me throw the bow of
the *Opal* boat into the lake
and any bits of wood you sawed off.
Or she'll never be satisfied,
and I'll never sleep again."

Bow Out

Austin and I trudge
over weeds to
the rundown house
looking worse
with torn screens
and trampled slope

Austin grabs the blue tarp
drags it into the house
clear of stink
clear of mist

we lay the *Opal* rowboat
bow on the tarp
load it with scraps of wood
even sawdust
lug it outside
wade into the lake
to dump it

we push and pull
the boat bow
further into the water

hurry to shore
when a gigantic wave
grows from the middle
of the lake

"Let's go!"
I yell

we dash up the slope
crouch behind the bench

the wave curls
sprays as it crashes
over the bow

swallowing it whole
dragging it away
until the lake shushes.

WHO'S LUCY?

Austin and I sit on the bench
in the weed strewn backyard
of the hopefully unhaunted house
stare at the glittering calm lake

"That was something, huh?'
shake my wet hair
out of my eyes

Austin's curved back sags:
"I don't understand what
happened out there."

"Pretty weird."
no one will ever believe me
except for Austin, Evie, and Blas
"So, umm, you live at a lake
and can't swim? That makes it tough
to make friends."

Austin rakes his fingers
through his hair:
"My mom doesn't want me

near the water. Sometimes
I sneak to the public beach
to go off the slide."

"That's tough."

he gestures toward the lake:
"Now I see why I'm not allowed
to go in the water. What does it
want with me?"

"Not you. Lucy wanted the rowboat."

"Lucy?"
Austin screws up his face

"The ghost."

"The ghost isn't Lucy. Lucy's
my mom."

LUCY EXPLAINED

I side-eye Austin:
"Your dad didn't call your
mom 'Lucy' the other day
in the rental office."

 "Vivian is her middle name.
 My grandfather, her dad, built
 the resort and lake."

"So your mom lived here."
jab my thumb at
the ramshackle house

 "Right. A long time ago."
 he nods

"And Opal was her dog?"

 "Yup. Like my dad said,
 Popcorn is a grand-pup or
 something of Opal's."

a drop of water wobbles

on the end of my nose:
"If the ghost isn't Lucy,
who is it?"

   "A wacko."
   Austin hangs his head

"Wait. You know when you said
you're not like Lucy?"

   "In the house when you were
   supposed to be helping me
   and asked a lot of questions."
   he snorts

"The ghost told me the same thing."
through Evie
I won't mention that part

   he bolts up
   "The ghost knows my mom?"

"Seems like it. And didn't
like her very much."

   "My mom grew up here. Doesn't
   go out much. She's the loner.
   She does office work with
   my dad and that's about it."

rub my worn-out arms:
"I wonder if your mom knows
who the ghost really is?"

THE MOM AND DAD
EXPLOSION

Austin and I wander to our dock
where Evie inspects Mr. Crunch

nothing to do but wait
for the Mom and Dad explosion

the slamming of the screen door
announces we won't wait much longer

the parents thunder down the stairs

"Are you boys all right?"
Dad asks

"We're fine, but we lost the dinghy."
I wave my hand toward the lake

Austin stares at the cracks in the dock
like he'd never seen anything so interesting
in his entire life
or he's waiting for mist to creep between
the boards

Mom's eyes flip from shock
to disappointment
to worry
her gaze takes in the cut on my chin
splinter infested hands
rope burns across my middle

Dad shakes his head:
"You didn't say you were on the lake."

I fold and unfold my arms

Mom points to the capsized speedboat:
"What happened to that?"

"It had a run-in with a raft."
rub the back of my neck

Evie dances with her blue lizard
singing:
"Jayce rescued Mr. Crunch."

Austin dips his head
I cringe

Mom reaches for Evie's arm:
"Careful, honey. We don't want
you falling off the dock."

"If I do, Jayce will save me.
He's my hero."
Evie beams like a walking ghost lantern

Austin covers a smirk
reaches out to pat my back

I don't feel like a hero

"You never should have
gone next door."
Dad's forehead scrunches
into a thousand wrinkles

I squirm in my skin:
"I guess."

the fact that I was brave enough to go
next door with a ghost hovering around us
rescue Mr. Crunch
keep Austin from getting on the bus
and get both of us to shore
canceled that part out

for me
not exactly for Dad.

THE AGREEMENT

Mr. Glaze screeches up
to our house in his car:
"You're a brave kid to go
across the lake after Austin,"
he says to me
after he collects Austin
bundles him in his car:
"You both could've gotten
killed out there. I don't understand
why that crazy guy who owns
the dollar store didn't see the raft?"

if the ghost can talk out of Evie's mouth
it can possess someone driving a boat

Evie, Austin, and I have
a silent agreement about the ghost

we make a pact with our eyes
Evie's with their edge of scariness
Austin's dulled to grey
but with a little spark way back in his head

we aren't telling our parents
about the ghost

not yet

or ever.

Three Reasons Not
to Tell the Parents

i.

the grown-ups would never believe us
why bother?

ii.

if they believe us
they'll pack us up
and we'll leave by dinner

iii.

I want to see if the ghost
will make another appearance
so I can ask it

why me?

A Haiku-Sized Dream

That night
I fall asleep
clutching my notebook
and pencil

force myself to dream
I'm writing the ghost a letter

I need answers
instead of counting sheep
I count letters

lots of letters
writing them
mailing them
sorting them

I fall asleep
scribble the note
fold the paper
shove it in the gaping hole
of the rusty
crusty mailbox:

Why did you choose me

to read your scary letters

Is it ghost radar?

wait by the mailbox
fighting the magnetic draw

steam streams from
the dark opening
I pluck the damp note
shake it open:

252 SANDY DEUTSCHER GREEN

Why did you choose me

to read your scary letters

Is it ghost radar?

you're not that special

you were willing to help me

anybody can

Who are you?

How do you know Lucy and Austin?

Why not talk to me?

feel a little deflated
like that dingy dinghy
it's not a special ghost sense

before I write:

Who are you? How do
you know Lucy and Austin?
Why not talk to me?

another note flutters in the mailbox
like a nervous butterfly:

you forgot to

and I wake up.

THE NEXT DAY

The Glazes

Mr. Tom Glaze
Mrs. Lucy Vivian Glaze
Austin Glaze
and little Popcorn

return our beach towel

Mom brings a tray of iced tea
and bowl of water to the deck

Dad and Mr. Glaze make golf plans
Austin gets to drive the cart

Mrs. Glaze fiddles with
the drawstring on her shorts

trying to look like she's not
trying to look at her old house

Popcorn yaps at the lake
and the house next door

"I'm sorry he's fussing."
Mrs. Glaze ties his leash
tighter to her chair:
"We never bring him to the lake."

Like Austin.
I plunge in:
"Austin says Popcorn's
related to **Opal,** the dog that used to live next door."

Evie clutches Mr. Crunch
Austin frowns at me
I'm not breaking our agreement about the ghost
I want to know the connection

Mrs. Glaze's hand flies to
her throat where she wears
one of Mr. Glaze's creations

necklace of
shimmering beads
white drops that
swallowed rainbows

Mom leans toward Mrs. Glaze:
"What a lovely necklace. What
kind of stones are they?"

Mrs. Glaze stutters

Mr. Glaze interrupts his
conversation with Dad:
"Opals!"

A WATERFALL OF
WORDS

Awkward silence
envelopes us
like a cloud

    "Mom, I thought we're not
    going to have secrets anymore."
    Austin says

Mrs. Glaze holds up her iced tea glass
sets it down
her hands flutter to her neck
like sparrows

    Mr. Glaze reaches for her hand:
    "Go on, dear."

Mrs. Glaze's words trickle
she tells us—
Douglasina

    or Doogie

lived across the lake

they went to school together
Doogie's family

guess that includes brother Mew

resented Lucy's family
for tearing up the sports fields
and building the resort

they never got along
Doogie was a quiet girl
never said much
but would leave nasty notes
for Mrs. Glaze to find
in her schoolbooks and in her mailbox

Mailbox!

"You gotta watch those quiet kids,"
Evie says
stroking Mr. Crunch's fluff around his face

Mrs. Glaze titters
and her words dribble—
they graduated from high school
Lucy was relieved
no more Doogie
Lucy always loved dogs
started breeding Maltese puppies
as well as working in the rental office
the resort became a big success,
her parents moved to Florida to retire
and left the running of the resort to Lucy

then Doogie sent her a letter
she wanted one of Opal's puppies
but Lucy promised them to others

and she gave one to Tom

who was the resort's caretaker
and they were engaged

Mom smiles at her:
"That's so sweet. Go on. It's good
to get things out in the open."

Mrs. Glaze picks up
the flow of the story—
that was the last straw for Doogie
Opal disappeared one day
from Lucy's dock
she heard the dog
whine and bark
over the water

sneak Evie a look

Mrs. Glaze's words gush
she tells us—
she rowed across the lake
and rescued Opal
from Doogie's house behind
the dollar emporium
Opal was barking from
the screen door in her kitchen

Doogie chased them back
in her rowboat
to Lucy's dock
but Lucy had run to Tom's house

waited for Doogie to show up
she never did

they found Doogie's rowboat
at Lucy's dock
and rowed Doogie's boat back
figuring Doogie wandered off

I have a weird feeling
this doesn't end well

the torrent continues
Mrs. Glaze tells us—
Doogie must've hit her head
on Lucy's dock
and slipped into the water
police found her body
determined it was an accident
but assumed it was Doogie's dock
since her boat was there

since everyone in Stanley
knew of the bad feelings
between Lucy's and Doogie's family
Lucy and Tom kept quiet

Mrs. Glaze looks like
she swam across the lake
and canoed over a waterfall:
"I've never told anyone else
aside from Tom knowing
and then Austin yesterday."

Mom refilled her iced tea glass:
"That's a big secret to have."

"It wasn't your fault. I don't think
Doogie's family would have made
it easy for you if they knew what
happened."

Dad shakes his head

"Your story is safe with us."
Mom says

"She was mean,"
Evie clutches her lizard

I think Mr. Crunch's head
will pop off
No wonder Ghost Doogie
is so mad:
"Is that why you don't
rent out the house next door?"

"We can't get anyone to fix
it up. They all quit after
a few days."
Mr. Glaze shrugs

Austin, Evie, and I
reinforce our silent agreement
with our eyes.

A Gift from Austin

"I have something
for you guys."
Austin reaches
under the table
hands me a lunch bag:
"I know you're leaving
in a couple days.
This is for you
and Evie on your trip home
and something
to remind you of Lake Lucy."

I glance into the bag
take out a handful of
wrapped candy

Evie and I laugh
"Thanks,"
we say in twin speak

two minutes after they leave
Evie grabs my arm:
"Let's divvy up the snacks

Austin gave us."

I pour out the bag
on my bed:
"What does Austin mean
by something
to remember Lake Lucy by?"

Evie shrugs
divides two neat piles
of candy

my fingers grope
the bottom of the sack

"Is that all?
I love these fruity candies."
her smile fades
as we lock eyes:
"Are you okay?"

This Turns into a
Can of Worms

I poke my nose in the bag:
"There's something else in here.
A note."
pick out a paper:
"It's from Austin."

I found this in the house when I worked
on the raft. Maybe Mr. Crunch can use it.

dig deeper
shake out
the leather wrist band Austin wore

Evie reaches for the crackly leather band:
"A tag with swirly writing is pinned to it."
she squints
rubs the battered metal:
"'Opal'. This belonged to Mrs. Glaze's
little dog."

she fits the collar around
Mr. Crunch's neck
buckles it:
"Cool."

something nags in the back
of my brain

"I know just how Mrs. Glaze felt
when Opal was lost."
she squeezes Mr. Crunch:
"Want to go for a swim?"

"I've had enough of the lake
to last me awhile."
scrunch my nose like
I ate a sour candy

Evie fusses with the dog tag:
"We can fish instead."

in the basement
I find poles Blas and I
used and bring them to the dock

Evie's busy rolling slices of bread
into marbles for bait

after we cast our lines
we dangle our legs over

the edge of the dock

"What a weird vacation."
swing my legs

Evie glances toward the house:
"You don't think the ghost
will come back, do you?"

"Naw. I'm pretty sure
Doogie has all she wants.
Austin and I threw every scrap
of Opal's rowboat in the lake."

"Pretty sure?"
Evie rests her arm on Mr. Crunch

my bobber disappears under the ripples:
"I've got something already."

"Not fair."

"Look."
I lean back against the bend of the pole

"Probably a shoe."

I laugh
reel in the empty line

"Need another bread ball?"

"This one's fine."
cast the line out again
the bobber vanishes

peer over my knees:

"Where'd it go?"
splash
I'm dragged into the churning lake.

FISHING FOR GHOSTS

I pop out of the water
gasping for air

"Jayce,"
Evie screams

something claws at my shorts
I plunge under again
the water temperature drops

use the fishing pole as a sword
swishing

    stabbing
    fencing in slow motion

the thing releases me

a thin crust of ice covers the surface
I crash through the shell
head for the dock's ladder

Evie balances on the edge of the dock

life preserver under one arm
Mr. Crunch under the other

the lake calms

"Quick, Jayce. Get to the ladder."

sputter when I
see it under the dock
smoky haze curls around the pilings
and reaches out to me

yell to terrified Evie
as she stares at a giant horse fly
forming from mist
above my head

more mist seeps through cracks in the dock
crawl up Evie's legs
she beats at it with the life preserver

out of the terror
the ghost letter
from my dream
appears in my head

> **Opal! Get her things to me**
> *not only the rowboat*
> *'her dear collar'*

I cling to the ladder:
"Throw Opal's collar into the lake."

Evie drops the life preserver
fumbles with the collar's buckle:
"It's stuck!"

as I pull on the rungs of the ladder
the horse fly thing inches toward me
I strike it with my free arm
ice crystals bite my skin

"Hurry! Try again."

mist curls around my waist
like a frozen lead belt
drags me into the water
I fight it
pop out of the water panting

Evie yanks the collar over Mr. Crunch's head
but it's caught on his thick fluff
"It won't come off!"
she sobs

hook my arm through the ladder
the weight of the lake hangs on me

my chattering teeth
grind my tongue
as my arms
slip from the rungs

an ice shield closes over my head
and I sink into the heavy water.

THE CHOICE

Bubbles tickle my nose and cheeks
I drift downward
into the gray soupy water
something plops into the water

Evie!
the ice cracks
a vortex of water
spins her

maybe the two of us can fight
this ghost-monster-horsefly together

blink the blur away

it's not Evie
not the life preserver
it's blue

Evie threw in Mr. Crunch.

Feeling Blue

The crushing feeling lifts as
Mr. Crunch spins
to the bottom
of the lake

Opal's collar on his neck

I kick towards the wavy sky
thrusting fists through the ice
burst out of the water
gasping great gulps of air

Evie tosses the life preserver
missing my head by an inch

she drags me to the ladder
crushing me in a hug
as we sit like stones
on the deck
staring over the lake.

LAST VISIT TO THE
PUBLIC BEACH

The day before we leave Lake Lucy
we visit the public beach
it's not the same without Blas
except Crystal busily buries her sister
up to her neck in the sand
and floats bob with bouncing and sliding kids

a tattered picture of a smiling blue head
with wispy hair
secret expression
is tacked to a pine tree
where Austin tripped me

"Wow, he can really draw!"
I pluck it from the tree

"Who drew that? It gives me chills."
Evie rubs her arms

"Blas. He left it for me."
I smile

"Blue Blas. That's my nickname

for him. Tell him hi from me
when you text him."
she runs into the waves

raise my eyebrow
Not sure about that.

And what about Noah?

Goodbye to Lake Lucy

The night before we leave Lake Lucy
Evie gives me a red, metal mailbox
the size of a small shoebox
she found at the dollar store
I set it next to my clock

the next morning
its flag is up:

Dear Jayce,

Thanks for rescuing Mr. Crunch. I'll always remember what you
did even though I had to give him up. I guess you're worth it.

Your sister,

Evie

Welcome to Lake Lucy
Wi-Fi Password: #!RELAX%$

tuck the paper in the notebook
with all the letters from Austin

we stop by the rental office
to drop off the key to our house
and pay the bill

Mr. Glaze hangs the keys on a peg:
"Austin, Jayce and Evie are here.
Come say good-bye. Austin has
something for you."

No, thanks. Austin gave us enough.

a chair scrapes behind the curtain
Austin shuffles out holding Mr. Crunch

Evie nearly faints
reaches out her arms:
"Where did you find him?"
she buries her nose in his fluff

Austin jams his hands in his pockets:
"I saw something blue on the trampoline
raft at the public beach with tons of
towels and deflated rafts and other stuff."
he shrugs:
"We gave him a bath in the washing machine,
and he took a spin in the dryer."

"He smells great."
she hugs him:
"Thanks for taking care of him.
I wish he could talk and tell us
where he's been."

I sure don't

she holds him up:
"His collar's gone."
she gives me a long stare
takes the elastic bracelet
Mr. Glaze made her
slips it over Mr. Crunch's head

Dad points to broken down boxes:
"Planning a move?"

"We're moving closer to Austin's cousins.
He'll go to school with them."

Popcorn pops out from the curtain
followed by the real Lucy
the parents chat

I hand Austin a paper folded
to make its own envelope
he slips it in his pocket
maybe Austin will email me
if he's ever allowed to use
a computer again

a temporary friend can be a permanent friend

after we leave
I update Blas
tell him I saw his cool drawing
he sends many emojis
he likes to talk in pictures

hope Austin will be happy in his new town
and Doogie the ghost
who let her jealousy make her miserable
can rest in peace.

ONE SPECIAL PUP

One special
Pup
And the
Links to her memory

were the keys
to helping Doogie to
rest in peace.

THE DOG IN THE MOON

On the car ride home from vacation
Mom and Dad listen to a book
blaring through the speakers
from Mom's cell phone

on the wrinkly face of the moon
a dog's head appears in its shadows
follows us down the road

wispy clouds tumble across the sky
smother the bright light of the moon
like a lantern that blew out

turn to Evie:
"All this started because
of a thirty second video
I took on Dad's camera."

"About that."
Evie lays Mr. Crunch
across her lap like a snack tray:
"I showed it to Dad. He says
it's the reflection of car headlights

in the windows."
she shrugs

Maybe
but the rest of the stuff
mist
rowboat
raft
nightmares
dog collar
ghost
ghost writing
writing a ghost

are real.

WHY YOU, JAYCE?

Evie glances at the parents
in the front seat:
"Why did the ghost write to you?
Why not me? Or Blas? Or anyone else?
What makes you special?"

Doogie the Ghost
gave me one insight:

> *"you're not that special*
> *you were willing to help me*
> *anybody can"*

"Wanted to be helpful, I guess."

she frowns:
"*I* like to be helpful."

flop my hand on Mr. Crunch's head:
"You *were* a big help."

"Like how exactly?"

"Remember when we were searching
for the cell phone and battery?"

"Yeah."
she fingers scratches on her arms
from diving into bushes

hide my mouth behind my hand:
"You—you were sort of possessed.
By the ghost."

Evie blinks
narrows her eyes:
"What?"

"Doogie's voice somehow
came out of your face. You—
she said to save Austin."

her face blanks
she clutches her throat
rolls back her eyes

I hold my breath

she shakes her head:
"Nope. Don't remember anything.
But I believe you."

>   *we're not that special*
>   *yet somehow unique*
>   *a tiny bit weird*
>   *a tiny bit freak*
>
>   *inquisitive twins*
>   *and one creepy lake*
>   *a sweet little pup*

a rowboat namesake

we rescued a kid
with help from a ghost
and made two new friends
I don't wanna boast

Evie's smile glows
in the backseat
as she brushes
Mr. Crunch's fluff

cell phone buzzes
Blas animated his blue head drawing
with a blue thumbs up

can't wait to find out
where we go next year
for summer vacation
maybe I can help
some(one) (thing) again

pull my Diamondbacks
baseball cap over my face
wait for a pleasant dream
to wash over me
like the warm waters of
Lake Lucy.

ACKNOWLEDGMENTS

This book is only in the hands of children because of the enthusiasm and passion of Dr. Jennifer Ikner Lowry of Monarch Educational Services. I'm grateful for her sensitivity and guidance in shaping this work.

A big thank you to Blas Madera with his amazing talent and perception in capturing the feel of the book and executing the cover. It's perfect.

Thank you to Andy Green for his huge contribution in finding the essence of the book and translating that to the cover and summaries.

Another huge thank you to Olivia Green for her keen eye in developing my website. And for her vegan ice cream.

Much gratitude to Gary Green for his encouragement, support, and for taking our family on that lake vacation all those years ago. Who knew?

I'm grateful to all the poetry journals through the years who have published my poems, given feedback, and helped me hone my poetry skills.

And to the memory of Karen E.M. Johnston, a wonderful writer, critique partner, and friend.

ABOUT THE AUTHOR

Sandy Deutscher Green's poetry has appeared in university, national, and international journals. Her children's work is included in *Chicken Soup for the Child's Soul*, *Highlights for Children*, and poetry anthology *Words and Other Wild Things*. Sandy is a member of the *Society of Children's Book Writers and Illustrators* and the author of two children's novels and two poetry collections. Before the pandemic, she served as the literature judge for her local *Reflections Art Program*. Sandy and her husband live in Virginia USA and have two children and four rescue pets.

Safety Hotline Numbers

1-800-RUNAWAY

nationalrunawaysafeline.org

If you or someone you know is hurting and needs help, call or text 988 or chat on 988lifeline.org to reach the 988 Suicide & Crisis Lifeline.

Internet Safety Websites for Families:
https://www.missingkids.org/netsmartz/home

Ghost Writers Reader's Guide

Visit www.monarcheducationalservices.com for the
Ghost Writers: The Haunting of Lake Lucy Reader's Guide.

Printed in the USA
CPSIA information can be obtained
at www.ICGtesting.com
CBHW011533230424
7406CB00009B/167